CHRISTMAS IN MY HEART
3

CHRISTMAS IN MY HEART

3

JOE L. WHEELER

REVIEW AND HERALD® PUBLISHING ASSOCIATION
HAGERSTOWN, MD 21740

Copyright © 1994
Review and Herald® Publishing Association

The author assumes full responsibility for the accuracy of all facts and
quotations as cited in this book.

This book was
Designed by Bill Kirstein
Cover design by Helcio Deslandes
Cover Illustration by Superstock/Currier & Ives
Type set: 11/12 Goudy

PRINTED IN U.S.A.

98 97 96 95 94   10 9 8 7 6 5 4 3 2

R&H Cataloging Service
Wheeler, Joe L., 1936—   comp.
    Christmas in my heart.   Book 3.

    1. Christmas stories, American. I. Title:
Christmas in my heart.   Book 3.
            813.010833

ISBN 0-8280-0869-8

Acknowledgments

"Introduction: Snow and Christmas," by Joe L. Wheeler. Copyright 1994. Printed by permission of the author.

"The Candle in the Forest," by Temple Bailey. Included in Bailey's collection, *The Holly Hedge and Other Christmas Stories*, Penn Publishing Company, Philadelphia, 1925.

"The Gold and Ivory Tablecloth," by Howard C. Schade. Reprinted by permission from *The Reader's Digest*, Dec. 1954. Copyright © 1954 by The Reader's Digest Association, Inc.

"The Jubilee Agreement," by Terry Beck. Copyright © 1990. Reprinted by permission of the author.

"A Christmas Ballad for the Captain," by William J. Lederer., Included in Lederer's *A Happy Book of Christmas Stories*, W. W. Norton & Company, New York, 1981. Reprinted by permission of the author and the Reader's Digest Association, Inc. (© 1960).

"Rebecca's Only Way," by Annie Hamilton Donnell. Published in *The Youth's Instructor*, Dec. 18, 1928.

"A Gift From the Heart," by Norman Vincent Peale. Reprinted with permission from *The Reader's Digest*, Jan. 1968. Copyright 1968 by The Reader's Digest Association, Inc.

"The Fir Tree Cousins," by Lucretia D. Clapp. Published in *The Youth's Instructor*, Dec. 18, 1928.

"Star Across the Tracks," by Bess Streeter Aldrich. Included in Aldrich's *Journey Into Christmas*, Appleton Century Crafts, Inc., New York, 1949. Copyright 1949, 1963 by Meredich Publishing Company. Used by permission of Dutton Signet, a division of Penguin Books, USA, Inc.

"The Christmas Nightingale," by Eric P. Kelly. Included in Kelly's *The Christmas Nightingale*, Macmillan Publishing Company, New York, 1932. Copyright reserved © 1960 Katharine C. Kelly.

"My Christmas Miracle," by Taylor Caldwell. Published in *Family Circle*, Dec. 24, 1961. Reprinted by permission of the William Morris Agency on behalf of the author.

"A Small Gift of Love," by Mary Ellen Holmes. Originally published in *The War Cry*, December 24, 1966. Reprinted by permission of The Salvation Army and *The War Cry*.

"Yet Not One of Them Shall Fall," by Hartley F. Dailey. Printed by permission of the author.

"The Story of the Other Wise Man," by Henry Van Dyke. Published as a book by Harper and Brothers, New York, 1895.

Contents

Health,
Peace, and
Sweet content
be yours. &

Snow and Christmas

Joe L. Wheeler

Why do so many Christmas stories feature snow? Why is Christmas perceived as somehow incomplete without it? Snow, it seems, is the longed-for icing on the Christmas cake.

Could it be that because in this ever more computerized world where we live, snow represents one of nature's wild cards? Its very unpredictableness and untamableness are sources of its attraction.

Could it be because snow is such a beautifier? Nothing that snow touches can possibly remain ugly. Only love beautifies more than snow.

Could it be because snow represents renewal, new opportunities, the chance to begin anew?

Could it be because it makes us think of skiing, ice-skating, sledding, snowmobiling, sleighing, all the winter sports?

Could it be because the Christmas tree is such an integral part of Christmas? And, of course, few living things are more breathtaking than pines or firs flocked with snow.

Could it be because when we think of Christmas services—concerts, cantatas, oratorios, pageants, midnight services—we generally associate them with bitter cold, with snow?

Could it be because snow is such an insulator (walling the world out and the family in)? Outside blizzards may rage with blind fury, but so long as those you

love are safe inside, the experience is something to enjoy, to revel in, to remember through the years. The Janus side of snow is a warm, crackling fire in the fireplace, a cup of hot cider or chocolate.

For Christmas is a time when many of our family memories are made—and so many of them have to do with snow:

"Remember the time when we were snowed in for a week?"

"Remember the time when a blizzard knocked out our electricity so that we spent the entire vacation huddled next to the fireplace?"

"Remember when the snow even stopped our travel, so that we had to spend Christmas in an airport?"

Each of us can think of such memories, each tied to snow. Could the Nordic countries' near monopoly on Christmas stories be attributable to the snow factor?

With all these questions in mind, I analyzed the first two collections of *Christmas in My Heart* stories to find out how many of them featured snow. The answer: 23 out of 33 (more than two thirds). Just think of the following stories, then ask yourself if you would have liked them as much had snow been excluded:

In "David's Star of Bethlehem," snow provides the desired isolation from Christmas; paradoxically, this very snow brought restitution of Christmas, family, and love.

In "Christmas Is for Families," snow is not physically present, but because a daughter chooses home over snow, it plays a key role in the story, anyhow.

In "Christmas Echo," snow is associated with both the tragedy at the beginning of the story and the heal-

ing trumpet duet at its close.

In "The Snow of Christmas," snow represents coldness, loneliness, and loss in the first part of the story; at the end, it represents restoration of the circle of three.

In "A Certain Small Shepherd," snow, by precluding Christmas-as-usual, opens the door of opportunity for a miracle.

In "A Few Bars in the Key of G," snow, represented by the 12,000-foot Berthoud Pass, separates knowing from not knowing, love lost from love regained.

In "The Christmas of the Phonograph Records," snow recalls the bitter cold and hardships of the frontier more graphically than any number of mere words ever could; and the juxtaposition of the alien element of recorded music to plunging winter temperatures and snow coalesces into enduring memories.

In "Delayed Delivery," the blizzard compounds the loneliness of old age, in this case reversing the norm by walling friends and loved ones out—and loneliness in.

In "Guest in the House," snow is not directly mentioned, but subjects associated with snow are interwoven all through the story.

In "Gift for David," there are three scenes, each framed with snow; the first one represents despair; the second, hope; and the third, affirmation and love.

In "The Why of Christmas," snow represents ordeal, pain, trauma, and struggle—coinage that adds up to the ultimate gift.

In "Bethany's Christmas Carol," snow is the extra ingredient that adds texture to the story, making the season seem real, and making being exiled to a hospital at Christmas that much more of a sacrifice.

In "Why the Minister Did Not Resign," the snowy orchard serves as the stage on which the two feuding families clash. But it turns out to be the healing place as well: the coming together, undoing generations of hate and rivalry by the simple act of walking around a snowy log.

In "Meditation . . . ," virtually the entire story is set in snow. It is a winter story from start to finish—a snowy evening marked the end of a relationship for both people, a spring snowstorm restored her sense of purpose, a blizzard bridged the way back to God for him. And snow brought them together again.

In "Running Away From Christmas," snow is implied throughout, but actually appears only on the road that transforms two into four.

In "The Last Straw," the depth of a little boy's hurt is measured by his willingness to spend Christmas alone in the snow rather than face a bad sibling relationship inside the house.

In "The Tallest Angel," the whiteness of snow and ice represents, to a little hunchback, something unattainable—that is, until a teacher is willing to use a golden key to unlock the door.

In "The Locking in of Lizabeth," the snow sifting down between the two buildings represents barriers between generations, and snow on the judge's coat results in the unlocking of three lives.

In "Christmas Magic," the snow sledding contributes to a magical day that unites a house full of semistrangers into lifelong friends.

In "A Father for Christmas," the entire story hinges on snow country terminology, wearing apparel, and equipment.

In "Stranger, Come Home," snow highlights the differences between two cultures half a world apart, and between two women divided by a secret that would always keep them apart.

In "Tell Me a Story of Christmas," almost all the stereotypical Christmas stories that the father tries to tell his daughter have to do with snow or snow country.

In "The Bells of Christmas Eve," both the snow of New England and the snow of Europe prove to be key ingredients.

The Third Collection

Christmas momentum continues to grow. *Christmas in My Heart*, book 2, sold out its first printing in only one week, mainly because some of the distributors who were caught short between printings for the first volume determined to avoid that mistake again.

I have rather unorthodox criteria for judging the effectiveness and quality of the stories. With Book 2 as with Book 1, when I received my advance copy I sat down and, pretending I wasn't me, read it straight through. And as with Book 1, I cried all the way through. I figured that if I as author/compiler didn't have any more self-control than this, then with all the other ol' softies out there, the book ought to do all right.

I continue to feel that the key criteria for inclusion in a collection is whether the story moves me deeply, makes me laugh or cry. It isn't enough that the story be well written merely from a technical point of view; it must have power as well. When one realizes that among the myriad Christmas stories not many have this crucial ingredient, then it's easy to see why there are so few good ones.

I also include only those stories that exhibit Christ-centered values, so that narrows the field even more.

Everywhere I find people who are looking for stories like these, stories with the potential to make a difference in the lives of their children, grandchildren, nieces, nephews, godchildren, and friends—and, of course, in themselves.

Book-signing events (30 in 90 days; in Maryland, New York, Oregon, Washington, and California) gave me the opportunity to interact with many of you and to learn more about what you look for in a collection, such as this. Interestingly, in most of the events I signed as many of the first collection as I did the second.

The audiocassettes have added a whole new dimension to my life. Many of those who came by for book signing during my visit to Southern California had first heard the stories on their way home from work. Unable to move in rush-hour traffic, they had fallen in love with the stories on tape.

You voted a number of these stories into this third collection. The following have been included by special request: "The Candle in the Forest," "The Gold and Ivory Tablecloth," "Rebecca's Only Way," "Star Across the Tracks," "The Fir Tree Cousins," and "The Story of the Other Wise Man."

The responses and stories continue to immeasurably enrich my life. So many stories have been sent that I remain in the enviable position I was in during the evolution of the first two collections: I have a terrible time deciding which ones to include and which to exclude. So long as this stage of affairs continues—in other words, as long as you keep me supplied with a stream of stories—just so long will we be able to publish annual collections.

I have taken occasional editorial liberties, updating words or terms that have become archaic or have acquired negative connotations.

Coda

I look forward to hearing from you, and do keep the stories, responses, and suggestions coming. You may reach me by writing to:

Joe L. Wheeler, Ph.D.
c/o Review and Herald Pub. Assoc.
55 West Oak Ridge Drive
Hagerstown, MD 21740

The Candle in the Forest

Temple Bailey

In each collection there has been a mandated item: "You must include this story." This story represents the No. 1 mandate of the third collection. It is an old story that had almost been forgotten. But here and there were those who, having once heard it, were incapable of forgetting it, for it had warmed their hearts through all the years.

I cry every time I read it.

It reminds us that wealth may be measured in many ways; so can poverty. Often, either is merely a matter of perspective.

What a joy it is to bring back from the edge of extinction such a wondrous story! It was written by Temple Bailey, author of "The Locking in of Lizabeth," Christmas in My Heart, book 2.

The small girl's mother was saying, "The onions will be silver, and the carrots will be gold—"

"And the potatoes will be ivory," said the small girl, and they laughed together. The small girl's mother had a big white bowl in her lap, and she was cutting up vegetables.

The onions were the hardest, because she cried over them.

"But our tears will be pearls," said the small girl's mother, and they laughed at that and dried their eyes, and found the carrots much easier, and the potatoes the easiest of all.

Then the next-door-neighbor came in and said, "What are you doing?"

"We are making a vegetable pie for our Christmas dinner," said the small girl's mother.

"And the onions are silver, and the carrots are gold, and the potatoes are ivory," said the small girl.

"I am sure I don't know what you are talking about," said the next-door-neighbor. "We are going to have turkey for dinner, and cranberries and celery."

The small girl laughed and clapped her hands. "But we are going to have a Christmas pie—and the onions will be silver and the carrots gold—"

"You said that once," said the next-door-neighbor, "and I should think you'd know they weren't anything of the kind."

"But they are," said the small girl, all shining eyes and rosy cheeks.

"Run along, darling," said the small girl's mother, "and find poor Pussy-purr-up. He's out in the cold. And you can put on your red sweater and red cap."

So the small girl hopped away like a happy robin, and the next-door-neighbor said, "She's old enough to know that onions aren't silver."

"But they are," said the small girl's mother. "And carrots are gold and the potatoes are—"

The next-door-neighbor's face was flaming. "If you say that again, I'll scream. It sounds silly to me."

13

"But it isn't in the least silly," said the small girl's mother, and her eyes were blue as sapphires, and as clear as the sea; "it is sensible. When people are poor, they have to make the most of little things. And we'll have only inexpensive things in our pie, but the onions will be silver—"

The lips of the next-door-neighbor were folded in a thin line. "If you had acted like a sensible creature, I shouldn't have asked you for the rent."

The small girl's mother was silent for a moment; then she said, "I am sorry—it ought to be sensible to make the best of things."

"Well," said the next-door-neighbor, sitting down in a chair with a very stiff back, "a pie is a pie. And I wouldn't teach a child to call it anything else."

"I haven't taught her to call it anything else. I was only trying to make her feel that it was something fine and splendid for Christmas Day, so I said that the onions were silver—"

"Don't say that again," snapped the next-door-neighbor, "and I want the rent as soon as possible."

With that, she flung up her head and marched out the front door, and it slammed behind her and made wild echoes in the little home.

And the small girl's mother stood there alone in the middle of the floor, and her eyes were like the sea in a storm.

But presently the door opened, and the small girl, looking like a red-breast robin, hopped in, and after her came a great black cat with his tail in the air, and he said, "Purr-up," which gave him his name.

And the small girl said, out of the things she had

been thinking, "Mother, why don't we have turkey?"

The clear look came back into the eyes of the small girl's mother, and she said, "Because we are content."

And the small girl said, "What is content?"

And her mother said, "It is making the best of what God gives us. And our best for Christmas Day,

my darling, is our Christmas pie."

So she kissed the small girl, and they finished peeling the vegetables, and then they put them to simmer on the back of the stove.

After that, the small girl had her supper of bread and milk, and Pussy-purr-up had milk in a saucer on the hearth, and the small girl climbed up in her mother's lap and said, "Tell me a story."

But the small girl's mother said, "Won't it be nicer to talk about Christmas presents?"

And the small girl sat up and said, "Let's."

And the mother said, "Let's tell each other what we'd rather have in the whole wide world."

"Oh, let's," said the small girl. "And I'll tell you first that I want a doll—and I want it to have a pink dress—and I want it to have eyes that open and shut—and I want it to have shoes and stockings—and I want it to have curly hair—" She had to stop, because she didn't have any breath left in her body, and when she got her breath back, she said, "Now, what do you want, Mother, more than anything else in the whole wide world?"

"Well," said the mother, "I want a chocolate mouse."

"Oh," said the small girl scornfully, "I shouldn't think you'd want that."

"Why not?"

"Because a chocolate mouse isn't anything."

"Oh, yes, it is," said the small girl's mother. "A chocolate mouse is Dickory-Dock, and Pussy-Cat-Pussy-Cat-where-have-you-been-was-frightened-under-a-chair, and the mice in Three-Blind-Mice ran after the farmer's wife, and the mouse in A-Frog-Would-a-Wooing-Go went down the throat of the crow—"

And the small girl said, "Could a chocolate mouse do all that?"

"Well," said the small girl's mother, "we could put him on the clock, and under a chair, and cut his tail with a carving knife, and at the very last we could eat him like a crow—"

The small girl said, shivering deliciously, "And he wouldn't be a real mouse?"

"No, just a chocolate one, with cream inside."

"Do you think I'll get one for Christmas?"

"I'm not sure," said the mother.

"Would he be nicer than a doll?"

The small girl's mother hesitated, then told her the truth. "My darling, Mother saved up money for a doll, but the next-door-neighbor wants the rent."

"Hasn't Daddy any more money?"

"Poor Daddy has been sick so long."

"But he's well now."

"I know. But he has to pay for the doctors, and money for medicine, and money for your red sweater, and money for milk for Pussy-purr-up, and money for our pie."

"The boy-next-door says we're poor, Mother."

"We are rich, my darling. We have love, each other, and Pussy-purr-up—"

"His mother won't let him have a cat," said the small girl, with her mind still on the boy-next-door. "But he's going to have a radio."

"Would you rather have a radio than Pussy-purr-up?"

The small girl gave a crow of derision. "I'd rather

have Pussy-purr-up than anything else in the whole wide world."

At that, the great cat, who had been sitting on the hearth with his paws tucked under him and his eyes like moons, stretched out his satin-shining length and jumped up on the arm of the chair beside the small girl and her mother, and began to sing a song that was like a mill-wheel away off. He purred to them so loud and so long that at last the small girl grew drowsy.

"Tell me some more about the chocolate mouse," she said, and nodded, and slept.

The small girl's mother carried her into another room, put her to bed, and came back to the kitchen, and it was full of shadows.

But she did not let herself sit among them. She wrapped herself in a great cape and went out into the cold dusk. There was a sweep of wind, heavy clouds overhead, and a band of dull orange showing back of the trees, where the sun had burned down.

She went straight from her little house to the big house of the next-door-neighbor and rang the bell at the back entrance. A maid let her into the kitchen, and there was the next-door-neighbor, and the two women who worked for her, and a daughter-in-law who had come to spend Christmas. The great range was glowing, and things were simmering, and things were stewing, and things were steaming, and things were baking, and things were boiling, and things were broiling, and there were the fragrances of a thousand delicious dishes in the air.

And the next-door-neighbor said: "We are trying to get as much done as possible tonight. We have plans for 12 people for Christmas dinner tomorrow."

And the daughter-in-law, who was all dressed up and had an apron tied about her, said in a sharp voice, "I can't see why you don't let your maids work for you."

And the next-door-neighbor said: "I have always worked. There is no excuse for laziness."

And the daughter-in-law said, "I'm not lazy, if that's what you mean. And we'll never have any dinner if I have to cook it." And away she went out of the kitchen with tears of rage in her eyes.

And the next-door-neighbor said, "If she hadn't gone when she did, I should have told her to go," and there was rage in her eyes but no tears.

She took her hands out of the pan of bread crumbs and sage, which was being mixed for the stuffing, and said to the small girl's mother, "Did you come to pay the rent?"

The small girl's mother handed her the money, and the next-door-neighbor went upstairs to write a receipt. Nobody asked the small girl's mother to sit down, so she stood in the middle of the floor and sniffed the entrancing fragrances, and looked at the mountain of food that would have served her small family for a month.

While she waited, the boy-next-door came in and said, "Are you the small girl's mother?"

"Yes."

"Are you going to have a tree?"

"Yes."

"Do you want to see mine?"

"It would be wonderful."

So he led her down a long passage to a great room,

and there was a tree that touched the ceiling, and on the very top branches and on·all the other branches were myriads of little lights that shone like stars, and there were gold bells and silver ones, and red and blue and green balls, and under the tree and on it were toys for boys and toys for girls, and one of the toys was a doll in a pink dress! At that, the heart of the small girl's mother tightened, and she was glad she wasn't a thief, or she would have snatched at the pink doll when the boy wasn't looking, and hidden it under her cape, and run away with it.

The next-door-neighbor-boy was saying, "It's the finest tree anybody has around here. But Dad and Mother don't know that I've seen it."

"Oh, don't they?" said the small girl's mother.

"No," said the boy-next-door, with a wide grin, "and it's fun to fool 'em."

"Is it?" said the small girl's mother. "Now, do you know, I should think the very nicest thing in the whole world would be not to have seen the tree."

"Because," said the small girl's mother, "the nicest thing in the world would be to have somebody tie a handkerchief around your eyes, so tight, and then to have somebody take your hand and lead you in and out, and in and out, and in and out, until you didn't know where you were, and then to have them untie the handkerchief—and there would be the tree, all shining and splendid!" She stopped, but her singing voice seemed to echo and re-echo in the great room.

The boy's staring eyes had a new look in them. "Did anybody ever tie a handkerchief over your eyes?"

"Oh, yes—"

"And lead you in and out, and in and out?"

"Yes."

"Well, nobody does things like that in our house. They think it's silly."

The small girl's mother laughed, and her laugh tinkled like a bell. "Do you think it's silly?"

He was eager. "No, I don't."

She held out her hand to him. "Will you come and see our tree?"

"Tonight?"

"No, tomorrow morning—early."

"Before breakfast?"

She nodded.

"I'd like it!"

So that was a bargain, and with a quick squeeze of their hands on it. And the small girl's mother went back to the kitchen, and the next-door-neighbor came down with the receipt, and the small girl's mother went out the back door and found that the orange band that had burned on the horizon was gone, and that there was just the wind and the singing of the trees.

Two men passed her on the brick walk that led to the house, and one of the men was saying, "If you'd only be fair to me, Father."

And the other man said, "All you want of me is money."

"You taught me that, Father."

"Blame it on me—"

"You are to blame. You and mother—did you ever show me the finer things?"

Their angry voices seemed to beat against the noise of the wind and the singing trees, so that the small girl's mother shivered, and drew her cape around her, and ran as fast as she could to her little house.

There were all the shadows to meet her, but she did not sit among them. She made coffee and a dish of milk toast, and set the toast in the oven to keep hot, and then she stood at the window watching. At last she saw through the darkness what looked like a star low down, and she knew that that star was a lantern, and she ran and opened the door wide.

And her young husband set the lantern down on the threshold, and took her in his arms, and said, "The sight of you is more than food and drink."

When he said that, she knew he had had a hard day, but her heart leaped because she knew that what he had said of her was true.

Then they went into the house together, and she set the food before him. And that he might forget his hard day, she told him of her own. And when she came to the part about the next-door-neighbor and the rent, she said, "I am telling you this because it has a happy ending."

And he put his hands over hers and said, "Everything with you has a happy ending."

"Well, this is a happy ending," said the small girl's mother, with all the sapphires in her eyes emphasizing it. "Because when I went over to pay the rent, I was feeling how poor we were and wishing that I had a pink doll for Baby, and books for you, and, and—and a magic carpet to carry us away from work and worry. And then I went into the parlor and saw the tree—with every-

thing hanging on it that was glittering and gorgeous, and then I came home." Her breath was quick and her lips smiling. "I came home—and I was glad I lived in my little home."

"What made you glad, dearest?"

"Oh, love is here; and hate is there, and a boy's deceit, and a man's injustice. They were saying sharp things to each other—and—and—their dinner will be a stalled ox—and in my little house is the faith of a child in the goodness of God, and the bravery of a man who fought for his country—"

She was in his arms now.

"And the blessing of a woman who has never known defeat." His voice broke on the words.

In that moment it seemed as if the wind stopped blowing, and as if the trees stopped sighing, as if there was the sound of heavenly singing.

The small girl's mother and the small girl's father sat up very late that night. They popped a great bowlful of crisp snowy corn and made it into balls; they boiled sugar and molasses, and cracked nuts, and made candy of them. They cut funny little Christmas fairies out of paper and painted their jackets bright red, with round silver buttons of the tinfoil that came on cream cheese. And then they put the balls and the candy and the painted fairies and a long red candle in a big basket, and set it away. And the small girl's mother brought out the chocolate mouse.

"We will put this on the clock," she said, "where her eyes will rest on it the first thing in the morning."

So they put it there, and it seemed as natural as life, so that Pussy-purr-up positively licked his chops and sat in front of the clock as if to keep his eye on the chocolate mouse. The small girl's mother said, "She was lovely about giving up the doll, and she will love the tree."

"We'll have to get up very early," said the small girl's father.

"And you'll have to run ahead to light the candle."

Well, they got up before dawn the next morning, and so did the boy-next-door. He was there on the step, waiting, blowing on his hands and beating them quite like the poor little boys do in a Christmas story, who haven't any mittens. But he wasn't a poor little boy, and he had so many pairs of fur-trimmed gloves that he didn't know what to do with them, but he had left the house in such a hurry that he had forgotten to put them on. So there he stood on the front step of the little house, blowing on his hands and beating them. And it was dark, with a sort of pale shine in the heavens, which didn't seem to come from the stars or the herald of the dawn; it was just a mystical silver glow that set the boy's heart to beating.

He had never been out alone like this. He had always stayed in his warm bed until somebody called him, and then he had waited until they had called again, and then he had dressed and gone to breakfast, where his father scolded because he was late, and his mother scolded because he ate too fast. But this day had begun with adventure, and for the first time, under that silvery sky, he felt the thrill of it.

Then suddenly someone came around the house— someone tall and thin, with a cap on his head and an empty basket in his hands.

"Hello," he said. "A merry Christmas!"

It was the small girl's father, and he put the key in the lock and went in, and turned on a light, and there was the table set for four.

And the small girl's father said, "You see, we have set a place for you. We must eat something before we go out."

And the boy said, "Are we going out? I came to see the tree."

"We are going out to see the tree."

Before the boy could ask any questions, the small girl's mother appeared with fingers on her lips and said, "Sh-sh," and then she began to recite in a hushed voice, "Hickory-Dickory-Dock—"

Then there was a little cry and the sound of dancing feet, and the small girl in a red dressing gown came flying in.

"Oh, Mother, Mother, the mouse is on the clock— the mouse is on the clock!"

Well, it seemed to the little boy that he had never seen anything so exciting as the things that followed. The chocolate mouse went up the clock and under the chair and would have had its tail cut off except that the small girl begged to save it.

"I want to keep it as it is, Mother."

And playing this game as if it were the most important thing in the whole wide world were the small girl's mother and the small girl's father, all laughing and flushed, and chanting the quaint old words to the quaint old music. The boy-next-door held his breath for fear he would wake up from this entrancing dream and find himself in his own big house, alone in his puffy bed, or eating breakfast with his stodgy parents who had never played with him in his life. He found himself laughing too, and flushed and happy, and trying to sing in his funny boy's voice.

The small girl absolutely refused to eat the mouse. "He's my darling Christmas mouse, Mother."

So her mother said, "Well, I'll put him on the clock again, where Pussy-purr-up can't get him while we are out."

"Oh, are we going out?" said the small girl, round-eyed.

"Yes."

"Where are we going?"

"To find Christmas."

That was all the small girl's mother would tell. So they had breakfast, and everything tasted perfectly delicious to the boy-next-door. But first they bowed their heads, and the small girl's father said, "Dear Christ-Child, on this Christmas morning, bless these children, and keep our hearts young and full of love for Thee."

The boy-next-door, when he lifted his head, had a funny feeling as if he wanted to cry, and yet it was a lovely feeling, all warm and comfortable inside.

For breakfast they each had a great baked apple, and great slices of sweet bread and butter, and great glasses of milk, and as soon as they had finished, away they went out of the door and down into the woods back of the house, and when they were deep into the woods, the small girl's father took out of his pocket a lit-tle flute and began to play; he played thin piping tunes that went flitting around among the trees, and the small

girl and her mother hummed the tunes until it sounded like singing bees, and their feet fairly danced and the boy found himself humming and dancing with them.

Then suddenly the piping ceased, and a hush fell over the wood. It was so still that they could almost hear each other breathe—so still that when a light flamed suddenly in that open space, it burned without a flicker.

The light came from a red candle that was set in the top of a small living tree. It was the only light on the tree, but it showed the snowy balls, and the small red fairies whose coats had silver buttons.

"It's our tree, my darling," he heard the small girl's mother saying.

Suddenly it seemed to the boy that his heart would burst in his breast. He wanted someone to speak to him like that. The small girl sat high on her father's shoul-der, and her father held her mother's hand. It was like a chain of gold, their holding hands like that, the loving each other.

The boy reached out and touched the woman's hand. She looked down at him and drew him close. He felt warmed and comforted. Their candle burning there in the darkness was like some sacred fire of friendship. He wished that it would never go out, that he might stand there watching it, with his small cold hand in the clasp of the small girl's mother's hand.

It was late when the boy-next-door got back to his own big house. But he had not been missed. Everybody was up, and everything was upset. The daughter-in-law had declared the night before that she would not stay another day beneath that roof, and off she had gone with her young husband, and her little girl, who was to have had the pink doll on the tree.

"And good riddance," said the next-door-neighbor. But she ate no breakfast, and she went to the kitchen and worked with her maids to get the dinner ready, and there were covers laid for nine instead of 12.

And the next-door-neighbor kept saying, "Good riddance—good riddance," and not once did she say, "A merry Christmas."

But the boy-next-door had something in his heart that was warm and glowing like the candle in the forest, and he came to his mother and said, "May I have the pink dolly?"

She spoke frowningly. "What does a boy want of a doll?"

"I'd like to give it to the little girl next door."

"Do you think I can buy dolls to give away in charity?"

"Well, they gave me a Christmas present."

"What did they give you?"

He opened his hand and showed a little flute tied with a gay red ribbon. He lifted it to his lips and blew on it, a thin piping tune.

"Oh, that," said his mother scornfully. "Why, that's nothing but a reed from the pond."

But the boy knew it was more than that. It was a magic pipe that made you dance, and made your heart warm and happy.

So he said again, "I'd like to give her the doll." And he reached out his little hand and touched his mother's—and his eyes were wistful.

His mother's own eyes softened—she had lost one son that day—and she said, "Oh, well, do as you please," and went back to the kitchen.

The boy-next-door ran into the great room and took the doll from the tree, and wrapped her in paper, and flew out the door and down the brick walk and straight to the little house. When the door was opened, he saw that his friends were just sitting down to dinner—and there was the pie, all brown and piping hot, with a wreath of holly, and the small girl was saying, "And the onions were silver, and the carrots were gold—"

The boy-next-door went up to the small girl and said, "I've brought you a present."

With his eyes all lighted up, he took off the paper in which it was wrapped, and there was the doll, in rosy frills, with eyes that opened and shut, and shoes and stockings, and curly hair that was bobbed and beautiful.

And the small girl, in a whirlwind of happiness, said, "Is it really my doll?" And the boy-next-door felt very shy and happy, and he said, "Yes."

And the small girl's mother said, "It was a beautiful thing to do," and she bent and kissed him. Again that bursting feeling came into the boy's heart and he lifted his face to hers and said, "May I come sometimes and be your boy?"

And she said, "Yes."

And when at last he went away, she stood in the door and watched him, such a little lad, who knew so little of loving. And because she knew so much of love, her eyes filled to overflowing.

But presently she wiped the tears away and went back to the table; and she smiled at the small girl and at the small girl's father.

"And the potatoes were ivory," she said. "Oh, who would ask for turkey, when they can have pie like this?"

The Gold and Ivory Tablecloth

Howard C. Schade

If this story were fiction, editors would reject it as being too implausible, too coincidental, to have ever happened. Yet these storm-induced events did occur, a number of years after Hitler's armies had ravaged Europe.

Of true stories of Christmas, few are treasured and reread more than this.

At Christmastime men and women everywhere gather in their churches to wonder anew at the greatest miracle the world has ever known. But the story I like best to recall was not a miracle—not exactly.

It happened to a pastor who was very young. His church was very old. Once, long ago, it had flourished. Famous men had preached from its pulpit, prayed before its altar. Rich and poor alike had worshiped there and built it beautifully. Now the good days had passed from the section of town where it stood. But the pastor and his young wife believed in their run-down church. They felt that with paint, hammer, and faith they could get it in shape. Together they went to work.

But late in December a severe storm whipped through the river valley, and the worst blow fell on the little church—a huge chunk of rain-soaked plaster fell out of the inside wall just behind the altar. Sorrowfully the pastor and his wife swept away the mess, but they couldn't hide the ragged hole.

The pastor looked at it and had to remind himself quickly, "Thy will be done!" But his wife wept, "Christmas is only two days away!"

That afternoon the dispirited couple attended the auction held for the benefit of a youth group. The auctioneer opened a box and shook out of its folds a handsome gold-and-ivory lace tablecloth. It was a magnificent item, nearly 15 feet long. But it, too, dated from a long-vanished era. Who, today, had any use for such a thing? There were a few half-hearted bids. Then the pastor was seized with what he thought was a great idea. He bid it in for $6.50.

He carried the cloth back to the church and tacked it up on the wall behind the altar. It completely hid the hole! And the extraordinary beauty of its shimmering handwork cast a fine, holiday glow over the chancel. It was a great triumph. Happily he went back to preparing his Christmas sermon.

Just before noon on the day of Christmas Eve, as the pastor was opening the church, he noticed a woman standing in the cold at the bus stop.

"The bus won't be here for 40 minutes!" he called, and invited her into the church to get warm.

She told him that she had come from the city that morning to be interviewed for a job as governess to the children of one of the wealthy families in town but she had been turned down. A war refugee, her English was imperfect.

The woman sat down in a pew and chafed her hands and rested. After a while she dropped her head and prayed. She looked up as the pastor began to adjust the great gold-and-ivory lace cloth across the hole. She rose suddenly and walked up the steps of the chancel. She looked at the tablecloth. The pastor smiled and started to tell her about the storm damage, but she didn't seem to listen. She took up a fold of the cloth and rubbed it between her fingers.

"It is mine!" she said. "It is my banquet cloth!" She lifted up a corner and showed the surprised pastor that there were initials monogrammed on it. "My husband had the cloth made especially for me in Brussels! There could not be another like it."

For the next few minutes the woman and the pastor talked excitedly together. She explained that she was Viennese; that she and her husband had opposed the Nazis and decided to leave the country. They were advised to go separately. Her husband put her on a train for Switzerland. They planned that he would join her as soon as he could arrange to ship their household goods across the border.

She never saw him again. Later she heard that he had died in a concentration camp.

"I have always felt that it was my fault—to leave without him," she said. "Perhaps these years of wandering have been my punishment!"

The pastor tried to comfort her, urged her to take the cloth with her. She refused. Then she went away.

As the church began to fill on Christmas Eve, it was clear that the cloth was going to be a great success. It had been skillfully designed to look its best by candlelight.

After the service, the pastor stood at the doorway; many people told him that the church looked beautiful. One gentle-faced, middle-aged man—he was the local clock-and-watch repairman—looked rather puzzled.

"It is strange," he said in his soft accent. "Many years ago my wife—God rest her—and I owned such a cloth. In our home in Vienna, my wife put it on the table"—and here he smiled—"only when the bishop came to dinner!"

The pastor suddenly became very excited. He told the jeweler about the woman who had been in church earlier in the day.

The startled jeweler clutched the pastor's arm. "Can it be? Does she live?"

Together the two got in touch with the family who had interviewed her. Then, in the pastor's car they started for the city. And as Christmas Day was born, this man and his wife—who had been separated through so many saddened Yuletides—were reunited.

To all who heard this story, the joyful purpose of the storm that had knocked a hole in the wall of the church was now quite clear. Of course, people said it was a miracle, but I think you will agree it was the season for it!

The Jubilee Agreement

Terry Beck

Unrelieved labor destroys: gradually, but with a deadly certainty, the sledge-hammering of unrelieved stress begins to take its toll, with premature death or disability looming ever larger on the horizon. That is why the Creator ordained Sabbaths . . . and festivals . . . and jubilees.

Terry Beck, the mother of six children, today lives in Mount Hermon, California, When I asked her of the story's origins, she confided that it was inspired by the Jubilees of her own mother.

She accepted my offer to participate in this introduction: "My mother was a pioneering woman in many senses of the word. . . . The greatest gift I received from observing my parents' marriage is this: That life is enriched by adventure, creativity, and boldness—and strengthened by commitment, support, and the freedom to be unique."

The Jubilee Agreement was signed the year I turned 6. Mama had been out of sorts for weeks. Tiny wrinkles suddenly framed her gentle green eyes and her glorious auburn hair lost its luster.

Nathan, her firstborn, was the second-grade star of King Richard's Deli, the top soccer team in the local league. Twice a week she would load 4-year-old Jordan, 18-month-old Ben, and me into the van with Nathan and his teammates. We'd traipse around the county to games, practices, support meetings. Mama was worn ragged.

"Mothers," she told Papa after an exhausting day, "should be rewarded with an occasional vacation all to themselves. A sabbatical. A Jubilee, like in the Bible. A chance to get away." Her voice lapsed into a wistful sigh.

Papa, a giant of a man with dark hair and warm brown eyes, walked to where Mama was folding laundry.

"Would that help you shake off this confustulation, Beth?" he asked, using one of the conglomerate words from Nathan's childhood. "Then a vacation would be good. The children can take care of me for a week." He winked at us behind Mama's back.

Nathan and I knew life would be chaos by the end of one day without Mama. But not wanting to quench the flush of hope that brightened her cheeks, we nodded.

Unwittingly, we'd consented to The Jubilee Agreement. The terms: Every three years, Mama was to take off a week. She could go wherever she wished, within a budget agreed upon by Papa.

The next month, Mama's spirits soared on a flurry of trips to the library and travel agencies. Flooded with colorful brochures offering getaways to fantastic resorts and cities across the country, she went into a frenzy of cleaning, mending, and stocking the freezer for a week. Our neighbor, Evie, agreed to baby-sit while Papa minded his pharmacy.

Papa, Nathan, and I became morose, silent. Papa, between his continuing romancing of Mama and obligations at the store, had never spent time alone with us. Now he was having second thoughts about the whole Jubilee concept.

Yet at the train station, when Mama kissed us good-bye with worried eyes and asked Papa, "Will you really be able to manage?" he commanded: "Go! We're going to be fine."

On the way home, he insisted we play his favorite game. Morgue. Everyone played dead and the last one to talk, move, or giggle, won. Jordan, the winner of all three rounds, got to open the gift Mama left for us on the kitchen table. Ecstatic "oohs" and "aahs" greeted the two-foot-tall teddy bear pulled from the wrapping. Mama had dressed his soft brown fur in swim trunks and tennis shoes, a reminder that her destination was a health spa just south of the Mexican border.

Tucked under the bear's arm was a card adorned with a blue-gowned angel wearing a cockeyed halo and blowing a slender gold horn. Inside were two messages.

On the left:

My Precious Children,

That I should leave you now, for this Jubilee, is hard, I know. But our separation is only for a short time. This bear symbolizes my promise that, unless an act of God intervenes, I shall come home to you. Talk to the teddy when you miss me and take care of Papa for me.

And on the right:

Darling John,

I'm hoping this will be a special time for you to get to know our children in a deeper way. Thank you for the gift of Jubilee. Be assured that neither time nor distance can keep me from loving you with all that I am.

Always,
Beth

Buoyed by the bear (immediately christened "Teddy Talkto" by Jordan) and Mama's love, the week soared by.

Back at the station, the mother who ran from the train into our squealing midst, was slimmer, tanner, and more youthful than the one we'd seen off. With her hair newly cut to frame her face, the once-too-mechanical smile now extended to twinkling eyes.

"How I missed you!" she exclaimed repeatedly, hugging us each in turn. She threw herself at Papa, who picked her up and swung her round, kissing just like in the movies.

Mama described her trip's pampering massages, swimming, and horseback riding. But none of it impressed us as much as the inner calm she radiated. By Monday, Mama's frantic schedule hadn't changed, but her attitude had. She went about her tasks with a smile and a song.

When Mama came from Mexico, we'd put away Teddy Talkto. Nine months later, as Mama and Papa went to the hospital, he reappeared, dressed in diapers, tiny T-shirt, and snuggling a purple rattle.

Papa phoned us from the hospital that evening to announce Laurel Christina's safe arrival. Ben and Jordan ran straight to Teddy Talkto with the good news. Nathan took the opportunity to explain how Papa, wanting to claim the first dance in each of his children's lives, ceremoniously waltzed around the house with each baby. Nathan picked up Teddy and held him cheek-to-cheek, gliding solemnly around. Entranced, we joined in.

When Mama came home, we once again put away Teddy Talkto, but not thoughts of the dance.

That Papa's older offspring should collapse in a fit of giggles must have mystified him as he waltzed round the house with Laurel the first day she raised her head. But he never probed our laughter. Quietly, smiling, he finished the dance.

Having survived the first Jubilee, we looked forward to the second. Papa admitted relief that Nathan and I were older, able to help more. With a smile, he reassured Mama not to fear. The Jubilee Agreement did not include a baby each homecoming.

Mama patted Papa's chin: "Oh, John, what would we do without Laurel?"

We kissed Mama good-bye for Jubilee Two, 40 miles of unrelenting desert in Eastern Nevada on a reenacted wagon train crossing of the Western Trail.

Before her car even pulled out of the driveway, we searched the house for Teddy Talkto. We found him mounted on Laurel's rocking horse, dressed as a cowboy with a ridiculously huge hat and red bandanna tied over his nose.

Our week went surprisingly smoothly. And Mama's? The weather had been unusually bad. Bleeding lips and legs blotched with bug bites were her most visible souvenirs.

Hardships aside, Jubilee Two had the same magical effect on Mama as Jubilee One. She was again refreshed, renewed as wife and mother; Papa's enthusiasm at her return assured us of their love for each other. The Jubilee Agreement, we concluded, was good for us all.

The years passed. Our family took yearly vacations, but it was Mama's Jubilees that defined our lives. During Jubilee, we learned not to take her for granted, as well as how to run the washing machine, load the dishwasher, and light the incinerator. We participated vicariously in Mama's travels and her love of plotting adventure added spice to the daily routine.

Mama spent Jubilee Three at Seattle's World Fair, leaving Teddy Talkto in a raincoat outgrown by Laurel (a clue as to what she expected in the Pacific Northwest).

For Jubilee Four, Mama made it to Hawaii and we found Teddy Talkto sprawled on a beach towel, wearing a grass skirt and a lei.

Jubilee Five and Nathan's freshmen year at UCLA were Mama's excuse to "do" Los Angeles. She spent Jubilee Six at a dude ranch in Wyoming and Jubilee Seven at the Grand Canyon.

Papa joined Mama for Jubilee Eight (right after Laurel married), celebrating in Acapulco the end of the Jubilee Agreement. With all of us wed, there was no one home to see if Mama had dressed Teddy Talkto in a sombrero or mariachi outfit.

Early the next year, Mama began to experience fatigue and stomach pains. Blood tests ordered by the doctor led to exploratory surgery. The final diagnosis of advanced cancer left us devastated. Papa, crushed, refused to talk about Mama's condition. His silence became her biggest concern. For months, she functioned normally, though slowly, putting her affairs in order. She spent time with each of us, laughing, crying, reminiscing. Loving.

Papa waited on Mama like a devoted servant, but refused to accept the finality of her illness. Distant even through the funeral and burial, he was tearless and detached.

In the months following, every joy and victory seemed muffled without Mama to celebrate, too. Laurel broke through her grief when she gave birth to her first child: Bethany Jubilee, named for the agreement that led to Laurel's own conception. But even holding his enchanting, curly-haired grandchild did not seem to penetrate the wall of pain wrapping Papa's heart.

Hoping to lift him out of melancholy, we agreed to congregate at the house for a traditional family

Christmas that year. Nathan's wife, Melissa, organized the oldest grandchildren into teams that took turns baking cookies, making fudge, and wrapping gifts. We decorated a magnificent tree with ornaments made through the years, went caroling in the neighborhood and attended worship services on Christmas Eve. But when Papa went to bed, we soon followed, too discouraged to rally for games.

The next morning, we gathered, subdued, for the grand gift opening. Jed, my eldest, played Santa. After opening all the presents, he spotted one more, a large box, tucked far beneath the tree. There was no tag. Puzzled, we asked Papa to open it.

Hands trembling, he pulled out the treasured Teddy Talkto dressed in flowing blue robe, cockeyed halo, with a slender golden horn tucked under his arm. Instantly, Nathan and I recognized the angel. Papa covered his eyes with his hand. Jed pulled out the card in Teddy's hand. I nodded for him to read:

My Precious Children,

That I should leave you now for this Jubilee is hard, I know. But our separation is only for a short time. This bear symbolizes my promise that, unless an act of God intervenes, I shall come home to you. Talk to the teddy when you miss me and take care of Papa for me.

Jed looked at me questioningly. He had grown up with tales of Teddy Talkto and the Jubilee Agreement,

but did not understand the significance of the card. Brushing silent tears from my eyes, I motioned him to continue.

Darling John,

I'm hoping this will be a special time for you to get to know our children in a deeper way. Thank you for the gift of Jubilee. Be assured that neither time nor distance can keep me from loving you with all that I am.

Always,
Beth

A groan ripped loose from somewhere deep within Papa. Shaking, tears streaming down his cheeks, he stumbled out, to the kitchen.

We sat in silence until one of the children asked a question about the first Jubilee. Breaking from our sorrow, we took turns retelling the childhood stories.

When Papa returned, he carried the tray of cookies and fudge that always followed the opening of presents, smiling bravely. "Forgive me," he said, voice trembling, "for trying to deny your Mama her final Jubilee." Then, grandchildren giggling at his feet, Papa picked up baby Bethany and gingerly waltzed her round the room.

A Christmas Ballad for the Captain

William J. Lederer

There is something about war that brings out the un-varnished person that is so often hidden by peacetime glaze. But even in war, one's true colors are often concealed, for a time at least, from those one daily interacts with.

So many of us, in peace or war, classify people as being "good" or "bad"; sometimes we are right, and sometimes we are not. With reference to "The Old Man" and "The Unholy K's," perceptions proved to be something less than reliable.

William J. Lederer, author of such World War II classics as All the Ships at Sea *and* Ensign O'Toole and Me, *and co-author of* The Ugly American, *remembers a wartime Christmas that was like no other. It was early in the war, and Lederer was an officer on a Navy destroyer. On the return home from the terrible battle of Anzio, the ship was torpedoed. Lederer wrote down this true story as a Christmas memory of the ship's crew and captain, and then sent copies to those sailors who survived.*

It was picked up by the popular press and quickly be-came one of the most beloved stories of the war. Reader's Digest *editors featured it as their 1960 Christmas issue story; more recently, it anchored Lederer's* A Happy Book of Christmas Stories, *published by W. W. Norton in 1981, and it was featured in the* Family Circle 1993 Christmas Treasury.

Mr. Lederer is still writing; in fact, when I last spoke to him he was getting ready to submerge from civilization until his next book was completed. A fascinating Vermont gentle-man, he has known personally most of the literary luminar-ies of the past half century. He concurs with Hemingway, whom he knew well, that an author who lacks kindness will never be able to write stories that are worth reading.

Captain Elias Stark, commanding officer of our destroyer, was a square-shouldered New Hampshire man, as quiet and austere as the granite mountains of his native state. About the only time the enlisted men heard him talk was when they first re-ported aboard. He would invite them to his cabin for a one-minute speech of welcome, then question them about their families, and note the names and addresses of the sailors' next of kin.

That was the way he had first met the "Unholy K's"—Krakow, Kratch, Koenig, and Kelly. They had ar-rived with a draft of 17 men from the naval prison at Portsmouth, New Hampshire. Most of the prison group were bad eggs, but the worst were these four sailors from a small coal-mining town in Pennsylvania. They had chests and shoulders like buffaloes, fists like sledgehammers, black stubble beards, and manners to match.

They had once been good kids, the mainstays of St. Stephen's choir in their hometown, but somehow they had gone astray. They seemed to specialize in getting into trouble together, as a quartet. All four went into the Navy direct from reform school. Within six months they were in serious trouble again and had been sent to Portsmouth Naval Prison.

When they were called to the captain's cabin, they listened to his speech with exaggerated expressions of boredom. Then the Old Man broke out his record book to note the names and addresses of their next of kin. He looked up inquiringly.

Krakow, the leader of the Unholy K's, took the initiative. Spreading his tremendous arms, he pulled Kelly, Kratch, and Koenig into a tight circle. "The four of us, sir, ain't got no family. We ain't got parents or wives or relatives." He paused. "All we got is girlfriends, eh, fellas?"

Captain Stark simply puffed on his pipe. Patiently he asked, "Would you give me your best ladies' names and addresses for our records?"

The Unholy K's glanced at one another.

30

Krakow said, "Sir, we don't feel like it's an officer's business who our girls are." He stopped as Kelly tugged his sleeve and whispered to him.

"OK," continued Krakow sarcastically, "you want to know who our best girls are, I'll tell you. Mine's Rita Hayworth, Kelly's is Ginger Rogers, Kratch's is Lana Turner, and Koenig's is Paulette Goddard. They all got the same address: Hollywood, sir."

"Very well," said the captain, "I will list those names in my records. Thank you, that will be all."

As soon as the Unholy K's got below deck they began bragging how they had made a fool out of the Old Man. Kelly started a bawdy song, and Krakow, Kratch, and Koenig joined in. Each man, in turn, made up a lyric while the other three harmonized. They had splendid voices, and with their choirboy training they formed a wonderful quartet. They sang four unprintable verses about the captain and why he wanted their girls' addresses.

Actually, the captain had a good reason for obtaining personal information about the men. He strongly believed it was his duty to keep their families informed on how they were getting along. So, once every three months, in blunt New England fashion, he sent a personal note written in a tiny, neat hand to everyone's next of kin.

For example:

Dear Madam,

Your son John is well—and is happy as can be expected in North Atlantic gales. If he shaved more often and cleaned his clothes more meticulously he would be more popular with his division chief.

I think highly of him as a gunner's mate and, with luck, you should see him in a few months. You will find he has put on 12 pounds, and the extra flesh hangs well on him.

Sincerely,
Elias Stark
Commander, U.S. Navy

In September, after a year in the combat zone, our destroyer went to the Brooklyn Navy Yard for a three-week overhaul. Almost all the officers and men went home on furloughs. Only the Old Man stayed on board the entire time, working alone, day and night. No one knew the nature of his apparently urgent business; but whenever we passed his cabin we saw him hunched over his desk, scratching away with an old-fashioned pen, while his cherrywood pipe sent up clouds of blue smoke.

We were puzzled also by the scores of parcels in plain wrappers that began coming to the Old Man before we sailed. It was not until much later that we would find out what they contained.

Meanwhile, our destroyer had gone to sea again, protecting convoys across the North Atlantic to England. It was rough work. Icy gales battered us; ships were torpedoed almost every night. We had little sleep and much physical discomfort. Everyone drooped with fatigue. Tempers became edgy, and there were fights. Captain Stark was constantly on the bridge, smoking his pipe and watching everything carefully. Despite the fact that his clear blue eyes became bloodshot from exhaustion and he stooped a bit from weariness, he remained calm and aloof.

If he knew how the Unholy K's were trying to destroy the ship's morale, he never mentioned it. It was their well-rendered ballads that did the dirty work. Everyone was afraid of these four bullies; but when they sang insidious songs about the ship's officers, the crew listened. Their lyrics were so catchy that a song rendered in the aftercrew's washroom would be repeated all over the ship within a half-hour. No officers ever heard the four men sing; but the results of their music were uncomfortably apparent.

The Unholy K's had one song about the hundreds of packages the captain had locked in the forward peak tank. The lyrics said that the boxes contained silk stockings, cigarettes, whiskey, drugs, and other black-market goods the captain was going to sell in England. They depicted the captain becoming a millionaire and retiring to a mansion in New Hampshire as soon as the war was over.

The crew began to ask questions: Why *should* the Old Man be hiding the parcels? Why *had* they been delivered with so much secrecy? It was even rumored that the Old Man was head of a black-market cartel and the cartons contained drugs stolen from Navy supply depots. But when the crew saw Captain Stark, tall, quiet, dignified, they knew in their hearts that the rumors were impossible.

In mid-December we shoved off from Newfoundland with another convoy. There were 62 ships in the group, many of them tankers filled with high-octane aviation gas. Almost immediately we ran into a gale.

The ships wallowed and floundered among mountainous waves. For nearly a week we had nothing to eat but sandwiches, and it was impossible to sleep. On top of this misery, we received an emergency alert and intelligence that the largest Nazi submarine wolf pack ever assembled was shadowing our convoy.

After a few days at sea, all grumbling and grousing stopped. We were too weary to do anything but stand watch, straining our eyes and ears for the enemy. Finally the storm slackened and the submarines closed in. During the beginning of the second week, hardly a night went by without the sky lighting up with the explosions of torpedoed ships.

Then, at sunrise on the twenty-fifth of December, as we neared the southwest tip of Ireland, our protection arrived—Royal Navy planes. The seas calmed and we relaxed; for the first time in what had seemed ages, the men were able to get a hot meal and sleep. All hands, except those on watch, turned in thankfully, exhausted.

Suddenly at 9 o'clock on this Christmas morning, the bosun's mate piped reveille. A wave of grumbling passed over the ship. We had all expected to be able to sleep in unless there was an attack. A few minutes later, Captain Stark's voice came over the loudspeaker. "This is the captain speaking. Shipmates, I know you are tired and want to sleep. But today is Christmas. There are special surprise packages from your families. They have been unloaded from the forward peak tanks and have been distributed throughout the ship alphabetically."

The news exploded through the ship. Men scrambled for their packages. Sailors sat all over the decks, cutting string, tearing paper, wiping away tears, and shouting to shipmates about what they had received.

But the four Unholy K's found no presents. They stood together, watching the others sullenly.

"Christmas!" said Koenig. "It's only an excuse to get suckers to spend money."

"Don't show *me* your new wristwatch," sneered Krakow to a young sailor who proudly held it up. "If I need a new ticker, I'll buy me one."

One happy kid came jigging up with a huge box of fudge. "From my girl," he sang out. "Now I see why the Old Man wanted her name and address."

"Hey!" said Krakow, grabbing Kelly's arm. "Didn't we give the Old Man *our* girls' names and addresses?"

"Yeah," said Kratch, beginning to grin slyly. "Rita Hayworth, Ginger Rogers, Lana Turner, and Paulette Goddard."

"Then how come we didn't get anything?"

"Let's go see the Old Man."

The Unholy K's, smiling evilly, went to the captain's cabin.

"Captain Stark, sir," said Krakow with mock respect, "we got a complaint. Everybody on this ship got presents from the names and addresses they gave you."

The captain looked at the four men gravely. "Don't you think that's pretty nice?"

"But we gave you names and addresses, and we didn't get no presents."

"Oh, you didn't?" said the Old Man slowly.

"No, sir, everyone but us. That's discrimination, sir."

"By gum," said the captain, standing up, "there *are* four extra packages. Now I just wonder . . ." He went to his bunk and pulled a blanket off a pile of parcels.

"There's one for me!" hollered Kelly, surging forward.

Captain Stark stood up to his full six feet and blocked the way. Reaching into the bunk, he handed out the packages to the four men, one at a time.

"Now, if you'll excuse me, I'll conduct Yuletide services for all hands." He went out to the bridge.

The Unholy K's ripped the colored wrappings. Krakow couldn't open his fast enough and took his sheath knife to slash the ribbon. Inside the fancy box was a pair of knitted woolen gloves. He tried them on his big red hands.

"Gee, the right size!"

There was something else in the box. It was a picture of a shapely woman in a low-cut dress; and there was writing on it.

Dear Joe Krakow,
  I knitted these gloves especially for you because you are my best boyfriend in the U.S. Navy. I hope that they'll keep you warm and that you'll have a wonderful Christmas wherever you may be.
                              From your best gal,
                              Rita Hayworth

Joe Krakow felt around his pockets for a handkerchief but couldn't find one. "What did you guys get?" he said, sniffling.

"Me?" said Koenig shrilly, "I got a wallet and a picture of Paulette Goddard! *From Paulette Goddard!*"

Kelly received a watch and an autographed picture from Ginger Rogers; and Kratch's present from Lana Turner was a gold fountain pen and a sentimentally inscribed photograph.

The Unholy K's shuffled around to the bridge where Captain Stark, his Bible open, stood in front of the microphone.

Krakow said, "Captain, sir . . ."

"Later," the captain replied bluntly, without even turning. He switched on the loudspeaker, announced church services, and read the story of the Nativity to all hands. Below, in the engine room, men listened, and in the chiefs' quarters, in the galley, in the mess compartments—throughout the ship, 250 sailors listened as the Old Man read the story of Jesus.

When he finished, he said he hoped everyone would join him in singing a few carols.

The Unholy K's pushed in on the captain. "Let us help you, sir," said Krakow urgently.

"This is not your type of song," the captain replied.

"Please, sir, the least we can do is lead the singing."

"Please, sir, let this be *our* Christmas present to *you*."

"A Christmas present for me?" mused the Old Man. "Why, yes, we'd all appreciate having a choir for the occasion. What shall we start with?"

The four sailors looked at the Old Man and then down at the photographs and presents clutched tightly under their arms. They gathered around the microphone. Krakow coughed; then in his deep bass he boomed, "Shipmates, this is Koenig, Kelly, Kratch, and me, Krakow—four no-good bums. Today is Christmas, and we want to sing you a special ballad." He paused, and wiped his eyes and nose on his shirtsleeve.

Krakow raised his hand like a symphony conductor, and the quartet began to sing:

> Silent night, holy night,
> All is calm, all is bright . . .

The magic of the holy music spread. Everyone on the ship joined in. The helmsman and the officer of the deck put their throats to the Christmas ballad. Even Captain Elias Stark, the granite man from New Hampshire, moved into the quartet, inclined his head, and, in reedy tenor, swelled the song.

> Sleep in heavenly peace,
> Sleep in heavenly peace.

The joyous music rose above the noise of the ocean and the destroyer's engines. During the third stanza an enormous bird soared in from the low-hanging clouds and landed in the after rigging. It flapped its great wings and made noises as if it, too, were singing our Christmas ballad along with us. My shipmates said it was an albatross. But, even though my eyes were filled with tears, I'd swear that it was an angel.

Of course, that was many years ago when I was still a kid. But even then I could recognize an angel when I saw one. As sure as my name's Joe Krakow.

Rebecca's Only Way

Annie Hamilton Donnell

One of the beauties of giving is that it is relative. The less you have, the higher the value of what you give; if you are extremely poor—let's say, an orphan—then almost any gift you give takes on the value of a king's ransom.

Annie Hamilton Donnell is little remembered today, but early in this century her work appeared regularly in popular and religious journals. Readers will remember her "Running Away From Christmas" in Christmas in My Heart, *book 2. However, no story she ever wrote has been cherished more than "Rebecca's Only Way." In recent years, it has almost disappeared from sight and memory. I hope that its reappearance here will give it a well-deserved extension on life.*

T he thin blue line wound evenly through the corridor and out of the big doors. Just out—no farther. At the first whiff of the blessed freedom of out-of-doors the line broke into 63 pieces, every "piece" a little free blue orphan. The silence broke, too, into 63 shouts. For an hour the 63 little lone ones would forget that they were lone, and be joyous little players in the sun.

In a corner Rebecca and Sarah Mary had their playhouse; they were "partners."

"I know somethin'!" sang Sarah Mary, bursting with the joy of what she knew, "about Christmas. THERE'S GOIN' TO BE DOLLS! A trustee said it. 'Dolls,' she said, just like that!"

"Oh!" breathed Rebecca. "But I don't suppose she said one APIECE—"

"She did! She said 'every orphan,' an' that's one apiece! An old lady left some money because once SHE wanted a doll an' didn't anybody know it. An' guess who's goin' to dress 'em."

"Oh, I can't wait to guess!"

Sarah Mary edged closer.

"A—live—dressmaker!"

"A live—WHAT?"

There was actual awe in Rebecca's voice.

"Dressmaker—in pieces o' silk an' satin an' TRIMMIN'S!"

Rebecca sat very still. She felt that beautiful Christmas doll warm against her little-mother breast. If she rocked gently—like this—and sang a soft hushaby, her baby would go to sleep! In its silky-satin little dress!

Sarah Mary was chattering on. "I was helpin' Ellen carry the lemonade in for the trustees. Somebody said, 'Sh—little pitchers!' That was me. They were afraid I'd hear, an' I did! The dressmaker is a relation to the person-that-wanted-a-doll-once; and she said—the dressmaker—she'd make the dresses for her part. Don't you hope yours will be sky-blue, Rebecca?"

"Oh, yes, sky-blue!" thrilled Rebecca. "Though red would be lovely, or goldy yellow, or green. If she didn't have ANY color dress, I'd love her," Rebecca thought, rocking her darling-to-be in the tender cradle of her arms.

For 10 days Rebecca thought of the Christmas doll by day, and dreamed of it by night. A dozen times she named it. Sweet—Love—Delight—Joy—a dozen beauteous names. The tenth day she settled upon Joy. Her little silk child, Joy!

The eleventh day Rebecca saw the picture. It seemed to start up out of all her happy dreamings and dangle before her eyes— "Look! look at me! Look at my dreadful little orphans!" And Rebecca looked with shocked and horror-stricken eyes. The picture stayed right there, dangling. Nights, too, she could see it. A visitor to the home had brought the paper and read to the children about the hungry orphans across the sea, who were glad for just one meal a day. How contented, then, the visitor had said, ought these orphans at the St. Luke Home to be with their breakfasts and dinners and suppers!

When she went away, she left the paper; and in it Rebecca saw the picture. A score of thin, sad little faces looked out at her. Such hungry faces! One smiled a little, and the smiling hungry face hurt most.

"They are orphans, too; I'm kind of a relation to them," thought Rebecca. "But I'm never hungry. Oh, never!" She could not feel herself that kind of "relation." One night she went without her supper, and lay in the dark on her cot in the row of little cots, trying how it felt to be hungry. If she hadn't had that apple between meals—probably those other orphans never had apples between. Perhaps if she didn't eat any breakfast tomorrow. But at breakfast Rebecca ate her bowl of cereal eagerly. She could hardly wait for the breakfast bell. It was terrible to be hungry! That night Rebecca dreamed of her Christmas doll, but it was made of bread. A bread child that she rocked in her arms! And a score of sad little children stood round her as she rocked, and the smiling one broke Rebecca's heart, so that—in the dream—she held her Joy-child out to her, and said, "You may eat her—my beautiful child!"

The picture first, and then the plan. Rebecca made that plan with sweating little soul—it was such a bitter, hard plan to make!

There was so little time left. Anxiously she watched her chance, but it was two days before Christmas before it came. She was sent down town on an errand, and as a special favor given permission to "look in the windows." That meant she need not hurry. She could do her own errands, too.

She was a little scared. It wouldn't be exactly . . . easy. A great automobile stood before a toy shop, and a lady was preparing to alight. She was going in to buy a doll for her little girl! Rebecca read it all instantly, for she was Rebecca.

"Wait! Oh, if you'd only just as LIEVES wait! I— I've got one to sell—I mean a doll for your little girl. With a silk dress that a real live dressmaker made! If you'd just as LIEVES buy mine—"

The small earnest face gazed upward into the surprised face of the lady. There was no doubting the child's seriousness of purpose, however wild her words sounded. The lady was interested.

"May I see it—the dolly you have to sell?" she said smilingly.

A faint pink color surged into Rebecca's cheeks, and deepened to red.

"I haven't got her yet. You—you'll have to trust me to deliver her Christmas. If you'd only as LIEVES trust me!" cried Rebecca.

"My dear! Suppose you come up here into the car, and sit down beside me, and tell me all about it."

"Yes'm—oh, yes'm, I will. It won't start, will it, while I'm getting in? I never was in one before."

On the broad, soft seat Rebecca drew a long breath. Then quite simply she explained the plan.

"So I've got to get some money to buy bread," she concluded wistfully. "Do you think a doll would buy quite a lot? A SILK doll that a dressmaker dressed? If— if you was going to buy your little girl a silk doll, would you think a dollar'd be a great deal to pay?" Oh, a dollar was a great deal! But a great deal of bread was needed. And bread had gone up; the matron said so. Rebecca set her lips firmly.

"I've got to ask a great deal for my chi—I mean, doll. An' I'm going to sell my orange an' stockin' o' candy, too; we always have those at St. Luke's Christmas."

The lady's eyes, gazing backward through the years, were seeing the crumpled pink face of the little girl who had not lived long enough for dolls or Christmas candles. "My dear," the lady said gently, "I will buy your dolly. Here is the dollar. Now shall I drive you to St.

Luke's? You are from St. Luke's Orphanage, aren't you?"

"Yes'm, I'm a St. Luke orphan, an' I'd like to be driven, thank you, but I've got two places to stop at first."

"We will stop; tell us where. You may start now, James."

To Rebecca, the "St. Luke orphan," that ride was a thrilling adventure, so thrilling that she forgot her two stopping places entirely; and the big car had to turn about and retrace its swift, glorious way.

"Are you afraid? Shall I ask James to go slower?"

"Oh, don't! Oh, I mean, please don't ask James!" Rebecca's cheeks were scarlet, her eyes like stars. "I love to fly this way!" Rebecca craned an eager neck, and shouted to the lady above the whir of the car and her whirring little heart, "Do you—s'pose—James—would drive clear—up?"

"Clear up?"

"Yes'm—to St. Luke's door, so they could see me, 'specially Sarah Mary. If James would just as lieves—"

"James would 'just as lieves,'" the lady said with a smile.

The fruitman's was the first stop. Rebecca stepped down carefully, and stated her amazing errand to him with perfect simplicity.

"Will you buy an orange?" she said clearly. "It will be a nice orange, I think. I'll deliver it Christmas morning, but if you'd just as lieves pay for it now—"

Over Rebecca's head the foreigner's eye caught that of the Lady of the Automobile, and some message appeared to travel to him across the short space—over

Rebecca's head. It was as if the Lady of the Automobile said to him, "Buy the orange; I will make it all right." She seemed a rich lady, and the automobile was very grand and big—and the risk was very small.

"If it is not too much a price," the man said gravely.

"Oh! Oh, just a—a loaf of bread!" Rebecca stammered nervously. "Could you pay as much as that? I need the bread—I mean THEY need—"

Was the Lady of the Automobile holding up 10 fingers? The man went into his little store, and came back. Into Rebecca's hand he dropped two nickels. And Rebecca never knew that the lady dropped two into his.

"He was a nice fruitman," Rebecca said, and added shyly: "an' you were ve-ry nice. I'm glad everybody's nice—I kind of dreaded it. I never expected to have a beautiful time!" She jingled her money joyously. "It must be quite a lot o' bread, it makes so much noise!" she laughed.

At a candy store the lady accompanied Rebecca. Once more a message flashed silently over the child's head. The remarkable advance sale of a Christmas "stockin' o' candy" was accomplished without difficulty.

"Why, so was SHE nice! Now I can take the money to the orphans," Rebecca cried. "I know the way; that visitor told us."

And to the whimsical fancy of the lady it would hardly have been unexpected if Rebecca had gravely asked if James would just as lieves take her overseas to lay this unique gift of bread before the hungry children themselves.

"I'm glad it will buy a lot of bread; they're very hungry orphans. One of them is smiling—I couldn't SMILE could you? But perhaps the orphans over the sea are courageouser. Than St. Luke orphans, I mean. I couldn't hardly WAIT for my breakfast—" Rebecca broke off at that shameful little memory. Oh, these other orphans had to wait!

At the Relief Headquarters Rebecca went in alone. She did not talk much to her new acquaintance the rest of the way back to the St. Luke Orphanage. And she had forgotten her desire to show off to Sarah Mary. It had come suddenly to Rebecca that it was her dear child Joy she had left behind her. A great anguish grew within her—the anguish of affection. Her JOY was dead.

The matron of St. Luke's had always maintained that Rebecca Dill was a very DIFFERENT orphan from the rest. The queer notions that child took! And now this notion to have her Christmas doll—how did she know there was going to be one?—tied up tight in a paper bag—

"If you'd just as lieves," Rebecca pleaded. "I don't want to see her. I mean it would be EASIER. With a string tied 'round the top."

But Rebecca was not to be present at the Christmas Eve celebration at the St. Luke Orphanage. She was feverish and so nearly sick that the matron decided she must stay in bed. It was Sarah Mary who carried her up the doll (her beautiful, darling child!) in the paper bag, and the candy and the orange. It was to Sarah Mary that Rebecca entrusted the delicate mission of "delivering" them all the next morning to their separate owners.

"Aren't you goin' to LOOK at it, Rebecca Dill? Not PEEK?" It was all very puzzling and unheard of to Sarah Mary. "Mine slept with me last night, right in my bed. I could hear her silk dress creakin' in the dark."

"Mine creaked, too," whispered Rebecca, though of course it might have been the paper bag. "She slept with me, an' I kissed her through a little teeny hole." Rebecca did not say that she had poured her anguished, torn young soul through that "teeny" hole—that she had cried: "Oh, my beloved little child, how can I let you go? Oh, my sweetest, never forget your mother loved you!"

On Christmas afternoon came the Automobile Lady to St. Luke's. She was a flushed and starry-eyed lady. In her hand she had a curious paper bag, tied at the top. Would the matron send it up to the little Rebecca-orphan, who, it seemed, was sick? Surely not very sick—

"A little feverish, that's all; children often are," the matron said. And the lady smiled gratefully at the reassurance.

"I can go and see her?" she asked. "Not just yet—in a few minutes."

Up in her bed Rebecca tremblingly opened the paper bag. But first she read a "teeny" dangling note.

"The dolly I bought for my little girl—will my little girl love it as I am going to love her?

THE AUTOMOBILE LADY."

And under the signature Rebecca found a tiny postscript—oh, a beautiful, dear postscript!

"If you'd just as lieves be my little girl—"

A Gift From the Heart

Norman Vincent Peale

What do you give to someone who already has everything money can buy? In our affluent society, this is anything but an uncommon question.

Norman Vincent Peale, so recently laid to rest, was for most of this past century one of the most beloved—and certainly most read—preachers in American. As pastor of New York's prestigious Marble Collegiate Church, he gained a national following. Later, he became the guiding spirit of one of the most cherished inspirational magazines we have, Guideposts.

But out of all his vast output, nothing is reread with more frequency—or tears—than this brief true story.

New York City, where I live, is impressive at any time, but as Christmas approaches, it's overwhelming. Store windows blaze with light and color, furs and jewels. Golden angels, 40 feet tall, hover over Fifth Avenue. Wealth, power, opulence . . . nothing in the world can match this fabulous display.

Through the gleaming canyons, people hurry to find last-minute gifts. Money seems to be no problem. If there's a problem, it's that the recipients so often have everything they need or want that it's hard to find anything suitable, anything that will really say "I love you."

Last December, as Christ's birthday drew near, a stranger was faced with just that problem. She had come from Switzerland to live in an American home and perfect her English. In return, she was willing to act as secretary, mind the grandchildren, do anything she was asked. She was just a girl in her late teens. Her name was Ursula.

One of the tasks her employers gave Ursula was keeping track of Christmas presents as they arrived. There were many, and all would require acknowledgment. Ursula kept a faithful record, but with a growing sense of concern. She was grateful to her American friends; she wanted to show her gratitude by giving them a Christmas present. But nothing that she could buy with her small allowance could compare with the gifts she was recording daily. Besides, even without these gifts, it seemed to her that her employers already had everything.

At night, from her window, Ursula could see the snowy expanse of Central Park, and beyond it the jagged skyline of the city. Far below, in the restless streets, taxis hooted and traffic lights winked red and green. It was so different from the silent majesty of the Alps that at times she had to blink back tears of the homesickness she was careful never to show. It was in the solitude of her little room, a few days before Christmas, that her secret idea came to Ursula.

It was almost as if a voice spoke clearly, inside her

this city have much more than you do. But surely there
are many who have far less. If you will think about this,
you may find a solution to what's troubling you."

Ursula thought long and hard. Finally on her day
off, which was Christmas Eve, she went to a great department store. She moved slowly along the crowded
aisles, selecting and rejecting things in her mind. At
last she bought something, and had it wrapped in gaily
colored paper. She went out into the gray twilight and
looked helplessly around. Finally, she went up to a doorman, resplendent in blue and gold. "Excuse, please," she
said in her hesitant English, "can you tell me where to
find a poor street?"

"A poor street, miss?" said the puzzled man.

"Yes, a very poor street. The poorest in the city."

The doorman looked doubtful. "Well, you might try
Harlem. Or down in the Village. Or the Lower East
Side, maybe."

But these names meant nothing to Ursula. She
thanked the doorman and walked along, threading her
way through the stream of shoppers until she came to a
tall policeman. "Please," she said, "can you direct me to
a very poor street in . . . in Harlem?"

The policeman looked at her sharply and shook his
head. "Harlem's no place for you, miss." And he blew
his whistle and sent the traffic swirling past.

Holding her package carefully, Ursula walked on,
head bowed against the sharp wind. If a street looked
poorer than the one she was on, she took it. But none
seemed like the slums she had heard about. Once she
stopped a woman, "Please, where do the very poor people live?" But the woman gave her a stare and hurried
on.

Darkness came sifting from the sky. Ursula was cold
and discouraged and afraid of becoming lost. She came
to an intersection and stood forlornly on the corner.
What she was trying to do suddenly seemed foolish, im-
pulsive, absurd. Then, through the traffic's roar, she
heard the cheerful tinkle of a bell. On the corner opposite, a Salvation Army man was making his traditional
Christmas appeal.

At once Ursula felt better; the Salvation Army was
a part of life in Switzerland, too. Surely this man
could tell her what she wanted to know. She waited for
the light, then crossed over to him. "Can you help me?
I'm looking for a baby. I have here a little present for
the poorest baby I can find." And she held up the package with the green ribbon and the gaily colored paper.

Dressed in gloves and overcoat a size too big for
him, he seemed a very ordinary man. But behind his
steel-rimmed glasses his eyes were kind. He looked at
Ursula and stopped ringing his bell. "What sort of
present?" he asked.

"A little dress. For a small, poor baby. Do you know
of one?"

"Oh, yes," he said. "Of more than one, I'm afraid."

"Is it far away? I could take a taxi, maybe?"

The Salvation Army man wrinkled his forehead.
Finally he said, "It's almost six o'clock. My relief will
show up then. If you want to wait, and if you can afford
a dollar taxi ride, I'll take you to a family in my own
neighborhood who needs just about everything."

"And they have a small baby?"

"A very small baby."

"Then," said Ursula joyfully, "I wait!"

The substitute bell-ringer came. A cruising taxi slowed. In its welcome warmth, she told her new friend about herself, how she came to be in New York, what she was trying to do. He listened in silence, and the taxi driver listened too. When they reached their destination, the driver said, "Take your time, miss. I'll wait for you."

On the sidewalk, Ursula stared up at the forbidding tenement—dark, decaying, saturated with hopelessness. A gust of wind, iron-cold, stirred the refuse in the street and rattled the reeling ashcans. "They live on the third floor," the Salvation Army man said. "Shall we go up?"

But Ursula shook her head. "They would try to thank me, and this is not from me." She pressed the package into his hand. "Take it up for me, please. Say it's from . . . from someone who has everything."

The taxi bore her swiftly from dark streets to lighted ones, from misery to abundance. She tried to visualize the Salvation Army man climbing the stairs, the knock, the explanation, the package being opened, the dress on the baby. It was hard to do.

Arriving at the apartment house on Fifth Avenue where she lived, she fumbled in her purse. But the driver flicked the flag up. "No charge, miss."

"No charge?" echoed Ursula, bewildered.

"Don't worry," the driver said. "I've been paid." He smiled at her and drove away.

Ursula was up early the next day. She set the table with special care. By the time she had finished, the family was awake, and there was all the excitement and laughter of Christmas morning. Soon the living room was a sea of gay discarded wrappings. Ursula thanked everyone for the presents she received. Finally, when there was a lull, she began to explain hesitantly why there seemed to be none from her. She told about going to the department store. She told about the Salvation Army man. She told about the taxi driver. When she finished, there was a long silence. No one seemed to trust himself to speak. "So you see," said Ursula, "I try to do a kindness in your name. And this is my Christmas present to you . . ."

How do I happen to know all this? I know it because ours was the home where Ursula lived. Ours was the Christmas she shared. We were like many Americans, so richly blessed that to this child from across the sea there seemed to be nothing she could add to the material things we already had. And so she offered something of far greater value: a gift from the heart, an act of kindness carried out in our name.

Strange, isn't it? A shy Swiss girl, alone in a great impersonal city. You would think that nothing she could do would affect anyone. And yet, by trying to give away love, she brought the true spirit of Christmas into our lives, the spirit of selfless giving. That was Ursula's secret—and she shared it with us all.

The Fir Tree Cousins

Lucretia D. Clapp

If gifts are merely perfunctory, of what value are they? To pretty Ann Brewster, who gave such gifts, not much; and to those who received them, even less.

But this Christmas . . .

Pretty Mrs. Brewster sat in the middle of her bedroom floor, surrounded by a billowy mass of tissue paper, layers of cotton batting, bits of ribbon, tinsel, and tags. She was tying up packages of various shapes and sizes, placing each one when finished in a heaped-up pile at one side. Her face was flushed; wisps of cotton clung to her dress and hair, and she glanced up anxiously now and then at the little clock on the desk as it ticked off the minutes of the short December afternoon.

"I'll never be through—*never!*" she remarked disconsolately after one of these hurried glances. "And there's the box for cousin Henry's family that just *must* go tonight, and the home box. Oh, Nancy Wells!" she broke off suddenly as she caught sight of a slender little figure standing in the doorway, surveying her with merry brown eyes.

"Nancy Wells! Come right in here. You're as welcome as—as the day after Christmas!"

"So you've reached that stage, have you, Ann?" the visitor laughed as she picked her way carefully across the littered floor to an inviting wicker chair near the fire.

"Yes, I have. You know I always begin to feel that way just about this time, Nancy, only it seems to be a mite worse than usual this year."

Ann Brewster stretched out one cramped foot and groaned. "Here I am, just slaving, while you—well, you look the very personification of elegant leisure. I suspect every single one of those 49 presents on your regular list is wrapped and tied and labeled—and mailed, too, if mailed it has to be. Well, you can just take off your coat and hat, Nancy, fold yourself up Turklike on the floor here, and help me out. I've an appointment at 4:30, and it's nearly that now. I'm not nearly through, but I just must finish today. If there's one thing I'm particular about, Nancy, it is that a gift shall reach the recipient on time. For my part, I don't want a Christmas present a week cold, so to speak, nor even a day. And somehow, I always manage to get mine off, even if I do half kill myself doing it."

"'Do your Christmas shopping early,'" quoted Nancy, mischievously, as she seated herself obediently on the floor.

"Yes; and 'only five more shopping days,'" Ann smiled ruefully. "Why don't you go on? Those well-meant little reminders I've had flaunted in my face every time I've stepped into a store or picked up a daily paper for the past six weeks. They have come to be as familiar as the street sign out there on that lamppost—and receive about the same amount of attention, too."

"Well, after all, Ann, it is a delightful sort of rush, now isn't it? I'm willing to admit that I'd miss it all dreadfully."

Nancy Wells looked about her appreciatively at the chintz-hung room glowing in the warmth of the open wood fire, and with its pleasant disarray of snowy paper and gay ribbons.

"My, but that's a lovely package!" she remarked, as Ann cut a square of tissue paper and measured a length of silver cord. "And what a clever idea that is! I should never have thought of using cotton batting and a sprinkling of diamond dust for the top layer."

"Well, you see, Nancy, this is for Cousin Harriet. She has everything anyone could possibly wish for, and she always sends me such beautiful things that I make a special effort to have my gift to her as dainty as possible and a little different."

Ann paused and glanced at the clock.

"My, look what time it is! I'll have to go. I wonder if you'd just as soon stay, Nancy, and finish up that little pile over there by the couch. They're for the fir tree cousins down on the farm."

"The fir tree cousins! Whatever do you mean, Ann?"

Ann laughed gaily as she stood up and shook off the bits of tinsel and ribbon from her skirt.

"Oh, I always call them that in fun," she explained. "They're Tom's cousins that live down in Maine. The idea struck me, I suppose, because theirs is the 'Country of the Pointed Firs,' you know. I've never seen any of them, but I've always sent them a box at Christmas ever since I've been married."

"What fun!" Nancy exclaimed enthusiastically. "How many are there, and what do you send them?"

"I don't know that I should call it fun exactly," Ann answered dubiously. "This buying gifts for people you've never seen and only know by hearsay is—well—not un-alloyed. Let's see—there are Cousin Henry and Cousin Lucy, then the boys, Alec and Joe and little Henry, and one girl, Louise, who is just between the two older boys. And, oh, yes, there's Grandma Lewis, Cousin Lucy's mother."

Ann ticked off the names on her fingers.

"Yes, there are just seven of them. Tom says they have a fine farm. He used to go there summers when he was a boy. He just adores Cousin Lucy, and actually wanted to take me down there on our wedding trip. You can't accuse me of procrastination as far as they are concerned, Nancy, for I always buy their things long before any of the others. You see, I usually know just about what I'm going to send each one. I hit upon a certain thing and stick to it as nearly as possible every year. It's easier."

"Why, Ann, you don't give them the very same thing year after year, I hope?" Nancy looked up in comical dismay.

"Well, why not?" Ann demanded a trifle sharply. "Take Cousin Henry, for instance. I usually get a nice warm muffler for him, because I'm sure he can—"

"But I should think—" Nancy interrupted.

"My dear, it's just *freezing* cold there! They have terrible winters, and one needs mufflers—and more mufflers! You can't have too many. Then I nearly always pick out an apron of some kind for Cousin Lucy. One can't have too many aprons, either, especially when she does all her own work. For Grandma Lewis, I choose a bag or something to put her knitting in. This year I found some sort of an affair for holding the yarn. I didn't understand it very well myself, although they told me it was perfectly simple; but I thought an experienced knitter like Grandma Lewis would know how to use it. Louise is just 16, so it's easy enough to select a pair of stockings or a handkerchief for her. As for the boys, Alec and Joe, I always get them neckties—they can't have too many, you know—and for little Henry a game or toy of some kind. Then Tom adds a box of candy. Promptly one week after Christmas I receive a perfectly proper, polite letter from Cousin Lucy, thanking me in behalf of every member of the fir tree household. It does sound a bit perfunctory, doesn't it, Nancy? Sort of a cut-and-dried performance all around. Somehow, Christmas is getting to be more and more like that every year; don't you think so? I must confess I'm glad, positively relieved, when it's over! I'm always a wreck, mentally as well as physically."

Nancy made no comment; instead she pointed with the scissors to a heap of large and small packages over at one side.

"What do you want done with those, Ann?"

"Oh, they go in the home box. That has to go tonight, too. I was just starting to tie them up. Do you suppose you'd have time to do them too, Nancy, dear? I know I'm just imposing on you. Just put the two piles on my bed when you've finished wrapping, will you? Then Tom can pack them after dinner. Now I'm off. Goodbye, and thanks awfully."

A minute later Nancy Wells heard the front door slam, then the house settled down to an empty quiet, broken only by the rustling of tissue paper and the click of scissors as Nancy folded and cut and measured and snipped. The fire burned to a bed of dull embers; and beyond the small square windowpanes, the snow-lit landscape darkened to dusk.

"There!" said Nancy, as she gave a final pat to the last bow. "And how pretty they look, too," she added, leaning back to survey her handiwork. Then she carried them over to the bed and arranged them in two neat piles.

"Certainly looks like 'Merry Christmas,' all right." With which remark, she put on her coat and hat and went home.

It was several hours later that Ann Brewster surveyed with weariness, compounded with relief, the empty spaces on bed and floor. The last label had been pasted on while Tom stood by with hammer and nails, ready to perform the final offices. And the two boxes, the one for the fir tree cousins down on the Maine farm, the other for Ann's own family in Michigan, were now on their way to the downtown office.

"And now that's over for another year at least," she sighed. "And I'm too tired to care much whether those boxes reach their destination safely or not. Twelve months from tonight, in all probability, I shall be sitting in this same spot making that very same remark. And I used to just *love* Christmas, too."

Ann Brewster (she was Ann Martin then) had been brought up in a family where there had been little money to spare, even for necessities. Nevertheless, Mr. and Mrs. Martin had always contrived to make the day and the season itself one of happy memory to their four children. No elaborate celebration of later years ever held quite the same degree of delight and anticipation shared then by every member of the family. Ann recalled the weeks brimful of plans and mysterious secrets that preceded the day itself, with its simple gifts and its spirit of peace and good will toward all. Now it was so different!

"Tired, Ann?"

A masculine voice broke in on her reverie, and Tom's broad-shouldered figure filled the doorway.

"Cheer up! The boxes are on their way, or should be shortly, and a few days more will see the season's finish."

"That's just it, Tom. We're losing the spirit of Christmas—the simplicity and good wishes, I mean, that used to be the big thing about it."

Tom whistled thoughtfully, and when he spoke his voice had lost its merry banter. "I guess you're right there, Ann. We're certainly a long way off from the old days of five-cent horns and candy canes. A lot of that was youth, of course, but just the same, this modern deal is all wrong. It's a selfish proposition, as I look at it. I don't believe I've ever told you, Ann, about a certain Christmas of mine, long ago. About the nicest I've ever known."

"Where was it? Do you mean at home?"

Ann looked up, interested.

"No." Tom's voice changed and a shadow crossed his face. "You know I never had much of a home, Ann. My parents both died when I was only a little chap, and I was sort of parceled out to various relatives for different seasons of the year. No, this Christmas I'm thinking of was with Cousin Henry and Cousin Lucy. Queer I haven't told you before."

"I knew you spent your summers there," Ann answered a little curiously, "but I've never heard of your being there for Christmas."

"Well, I was, and I've never forgotten it. It was my first glimpse of what a real homey Christmas can be. The tree was just a homemade affair—that is, the trimmings. We cut the tree ourselves, a beautiful slender fir, and hauled it down on a sled from the hill back of the house. We popped corn and made wreaths, strung cranberries, and cut stars out of colored paper. And I tell you that tree was pretty—it wasn't glittering with ornaments and blazing with candles or electric lights."

"Did you have presents?" asked Ann.

"Yes, I remember Cousin Henry gave me a pair of homemade snowshoes. Grandma Lewis had knit some red wristlets for me, and Cousin Lucy a cap to match. I was the happiest boy in the State of Maine!"

Tom paused a moment. "But somehow, Ann, what I remember most was the spirit of the day itself. Cousin Lucy had worked hard, I know, and in the evening had a lot of the neighbors in; but she was the life of the crowd. Ann, I'd like you to meet and really know Cousin Lucy. I wish she'd ask us to visit them sometime."

"Somehow, I never supposed—" Ann began hesitatingly.

"Supposed what?" Tom asked.

"Well, I guess I never gave your fir tree cousins much thought, Tom. I didn't think you cared particularly. You've never talked much about them nor made any effort to—"

"Yes, I know," Tom broke in, "and more's the shame to me, too. It's queer sometimes, that, no matter how much you may think of people, you just sort of drift apart. But you'd better get to bed now, Ann; you look tired to death."

* * * * *

The Thomas Brewsters faced each other across the breakfast table the morning after New Year's. There was a pile of letters beside Ann's plate.

"I know exactly what's in every one of these missives," she sighed.

Tom smiled as he opened his morning paper.

There was a silence for several minutes while Ann slowly slit the seals one by one. She picked up a square white envelope that bore her father's well-known handwriting, and a minute later a sudden exclamation made Tom look up.

"Why, Tom—Tom Brewster!"

Ann's eyes glanced down the single page; then she began to read aloud:

My dear Ann:

Perhaps you won't remember it, but you gave me a muffler for Christmas once long ago, when you were a very little girl. You picked it out yourself, and I'll say this—that you showed remarkably good taste. That muffler, or what's left of it, is tucked away somewhere in the attic now. The one you sent this year gives me almost as much pleasure as did that other one, although I suppose I'll have to concede that these new styles are really prettier (but not any warmer or more useful) than the old. Your mother thinks they must be coming back into favor again, but I don't care whether they are or not. They're warm and they help keep a clean collar clean. For my part, I'm glad we're getting away from the showy Christmases of the last few years and down to a simpler, saner giving and receiving.

Lots of love and thanks to you and Tom.

Father.

Ann drew forth a small folded sheet that had been tucked inside the other one. It read:

Dear Ann,

I'm just going to add a line to put in with your father's, for we have a houseful of company and there's no time now for a real letter. Your box this year, although something of a surprise, was nonetheless welcome. I have thought for several years that we ought all of us to give simpler gifts. A remembrance, no matter how small, if carefully and thoughtfully chosen to meet the need or desire of the recipient, carries with it more of the real Christmas spirit than the costliest gift or one chosen at random. I don't know when I've had an apron given me before! I began to think they had gone out of fashion. I put yours right on, and your father said it made him think of when you children were little. The boys will write you themselves, but I'll just say that Ned and Harold both remarked that they were glad you sent them neckties. (You know we've always tried to think up something different, with the result that both are rather low on that article.) We've had lots of fun with Hugh's game. He confided to me that he'd been hoping somebody would give him one. So you see, Ann, dear, we are all pleased with our things and send you our grateful thanks. Love to you both from

Mother.

P.S. I was afraid my letter telling of your Aunt Cordelia's arrival had not reached you in time, but I need not have worried. She was much taken with that case for holding her yarn. She'd had one and lost it. And Katy was real pleased with that pretty handkerchief.

With a hand that trembled a little, and with burning cheeks, Ann drew forth the last letter in the pile. It was postmarked Maine, and contained two plain lined sheets, tablet size.

"This is from Cousin Lucy," Ann began, a queer little note creeping into her voice:

My dear Ann:
    When we opened your box on Christmas morning, I thought I had never seen anything so attractive. Seals and ribbons and greetings may not mean so much, perhaps, to you city people; but for us isolated ones, they add a great deal to our enjoyment and appreciation. Your gifts fulfilled certain long-felt desires, one or two of which I suspect are older than you are, Ann. Perhaps you cannot understand the joy of receiving something you've always wanted, yet did not really need. I am writing with my beautiful pin before me on the table. You see, it is the first one—the first really nice pin—I've ever owned. That is fulfilled desire number one. The second is the sight of your Cousin Henry enjoying a bit of leisure before the fire with his new book. I suppose Tom may have told you that once, as a young man, your Cousin Henry made this very trip to the headwaters of the Peace River. So few new and worth-while books find their way to us. Louise and the boys will write later, so I'll only say that Alec actually takes his big

flashlight to bed with him; Joe is inordinately proud of that safety razor; and as for little Henry—well, his father and I both feel that we ought to thank you on our own behalf, for all our efforts to make an out-of-door lad of him seem to have failed hitherto. He is the student of the family, but the new skates lure him outside and help to strike the proper balance. Louise loves her beaded bag, as, indeed what girl wouldn't? And as for Grandma Lewis, she fairly flaunts that bit of rose point. She confided to me that at 80 years she had at last given up all hope of ever possessing a piece of real lace!

I have written a long letter, but I doubt if, after all, I've really succeeded in expressing even a small part of our appreciation to you and Tom for your carefully chosen gifts. To feel that a certain thing has been chosen especially for you—to fit your own individuality and particular desire, if not always need—this, it has always seemed to me, is the true spirit of Christmas. And I think you have found it, Ann. Before closing I want to ask if you and Tom can't arrange to make us a visit this summer?

Wishing you both a Happy New Year,
Lovingly,
Cousin Lucy.

Ann Brewster laid down the letter with something that was half a sob and half a laugh. "I'm just too ashamed to live!"

"Why, what's the matter, Ann?" Tom looked puzzled.

"Cousin Lucy speaks of my 'carefully chosen gifts.' And they weren't, at all. They weren't even meant for any of them. You see," Ann swallowed the lump in her throat, "I've always just chosen their things at random. Yes, I have, Tom. One of those Christmas obligations you spoke of the other night, to be disposed of with as little time and effort as possible. And then last week, when I was hurrying to get everything off, Nancy Wells came over and I left a lot of things for her to finish wrapping while I dashed off to the dressmaker's. And I suppose, in some way, I got the fir tree cousins' and the home pile mixed."

Tom pushed back his chair from the table.

"Seems to me, Ann dear, that we've had the answer to our query, 'What's wrong with Christmas?' You've sort of stumbled upon the truth this year, but—"

Tom stopped, whistling thoughtfully as he drew on his overcoat. There was a misty light in Ann's eyes as she stood beside him.

"When will you have your vacation, Tom?"

"August, probably."

"Well, we're going to spend it with our fir tree cousins! And, Tom, I can hardly wait!"

Star Across the Tracks

Bess Streeter Aldrich

"The wrong side of the tracks"—what an image that phrase conjures! Even in America, sad to say, those six words carry loaded freight: that anyone from the unfavored side is already prejudged, presorted, and predetermined. Perhaps "Can anything good come out of Nazareth" was an earlier equivalent of "living on the wrong side of the tracks."

Bess Streeter Aldrich (best known for her best-selling A Lantern in Her Hand *and* A White Bird Flying*), along with Willa Cather, attempted to recreate in words just what it took for women to survive in Plains America. "Star Across the Tracks" is one of her most unforgettable short stories. In addition, it is one of Penny Estes Wheeler's (my revered editor) favorite Christmas stories.*

Mr. Harm Kurtz sat in the kitchen with his feet in the oven and discussed the world; that is to say, his own small world. His audience, shifting back and forth between the pantry and the kitchen sink, caused the orator's voice to rise and fall with its coming and going.

The audience was mamma. She was the bell upon which the clapper of his verbal output always struck. As she never stopped moving about at her housework during these nightly discourses, one might have said facetiously that she was his Roaming Forum.

Pa Kurtz was slight and wiry, all muscle and bounce. His wife had avoirdupois to spare and her leisurely walk was what is known in common parlance as a waddle. She wore her hair combed high, brushed tightly up at the back and sides, where it ended in a hard knot on top of her head. When movie stars and cafe society took it up, mamma said she had beat them to it by 35 years.

The Kurtzes lived in a little brown house on Mill Street, which meandered its unpaved way along a creek bed. The town, having been laid out by the founding fathers on this once-flowing but now long-dried creek, was called River City.

For three days of his working week pa's narrow world held sundry tasks: plowing gardens, cutting alfalfa, hauling lumber from the mill. For the other three days he was engaged permanently as a handyman by the families of Scott, Dillingham, and Porter, who lived on High View Drive, far away from Mill Street, geographically, economically, socially. And what mamma hadn't learned about the Scott, Dillingham, and Porter domestic establishments in the last few years wasn't worth knowing.

Early in his labors for the three families, pa had summed them up to mamma in one sweeping statement: "The Scotts . . . him I like and her I don't like. The Dillinghams . . . her I like and him I don't like. The Porters . . . both I don't like."

50

The Porters' house was brick colonial. The Scotts' was a rambling stone of the ranch type. The Dillinghams' had no classification, but was both brick and stone, to say nothing of stained shingles, lumber, tile, glass bricks, and stucco.

The Porters had four children of school age. Also they had long curving rows of evergreens in which the grackles settled with raucous glee as though to outvie the family's noise. The grackles—and for all pa knew, maybe the young folks also—drove Mrs. Porter wild, but pa rather liked the birds. They sounded so country-like, and he had never grown away from the farm.

Mr. Porter was a lawyer and a councilman. Mrs. Porter was a member of the Garden Club and knew practically all there was to know about flora and fauna. She went in for formal beds of flowers, rectangles, and half-moons, containing tulips and daffodils in the spring and dahlias and asters later. She ruled pa with iron efficiency. With a wave of her hand she might say: "Mr. Kurtz, I think I'll have the beds farther apart this year."

And pa, telling mamma about it at night, would sneer: "Just like they was the springs-and-mattress kind you can shove around on casters."

Mrs. Scott went to the other extreme. She knew the least about vegetation of anyone who had ever come under pa's scrutiny. Assuredly he was his own boss there. Each spring she tossed him several dozen packages of seeds as though she dared him to do his worst. Once he had found rutabaga and spinach among the packages of zinnias and nasturtiums. But pa couldn't be too hard on her, for she had a little crippled son who took most of her time. And he liked the fresh-colored packages every year and the feel of the warm moist earth when he put in the seeds. The head of the house was a doctor and if he happened to drive in while pa was there, he stopped and joked a bit.

The Dillinghams' yard was pa's favorite. The back of it was not only informal, it was woodsy. Mrs. Dillingham told pa she had been raised on a farm and that the end of the yard reminded her of the grove back of her old home. She had no children and often she came out to stand around talking to pa or brought her gloves and worked with him.

"Poor thing! Lonesome," mamma said at once when he was telling her.

Mrs. Dillingham had pa set out wild crab apple and ferns and plum trees, little crooked ones, so it would "look natural." Several times she had driven him out to the country and they had brought back shooting stars and swamp candle, Dutchman's-breeches and wood violets. Pa's hand with the little wild flowers was as tender as the hand of God.

When Mr. Dillingham came home from his big department store, he was loud and officious, sometimes critical of what had been done.

In winter, the work for the High View homes was just as hard and far less interesting. Storm windows, snow on long driveways, basements to be cleaned. It was always good to get home and sit with his tired, wet feet in the oven and tell the day's experiences to mamma. There was something very comforting about mamma, her consoling "Oh, think nothing of it," or her sympathetic clucking of "Tsk . . . tsk . . . them women, with their cars and their clubs!"

Tonight there was more than usual to tell, for there had been great goings on up in High View. Tomorrow night was Christmas Eve and in preparation for the annual prizes given by the federated civic clubs, his three families had gone in for elaborate outdoor decorations.

There was unspoken rivalry among the three houses, too. Pa could sense it. Mrs. Porter had asked him offhandedly, as though it were a matter of extreme unconcern, what the two other families were planning to do. And Mr. Dillingham had asked the same thing, but bluntly. You couldn't catch pa that way, though, he reminded mamma with great glee. "Slippery as a eel!" Had just answered that the others seemed to be hitchin' up a lot of wiring.

But pa had known all along what each one was doing. And tomorrow night everybody would know. The Porters had long strings of blue lights, which they were carrying out into the evergreens, as though bluebirds, instead of black ones, were settling there to stay through Christmas.

The Dillinghams had gone in for reindeer. They had ordered them made from plyboard at the mill, and tonight the eight deer, with artificial snow all over them, were prancing up the porch steps, while a searchlight on the ground threw the group into relief.

The Scotts, whose house was not so high as the others, had a fat Santa on the roof with one foot in the chimney. In a near-by dormer window there was a phonograph which would play Jingle Bells, so that the song seemingly came from the old fellow himself. It

had made the little crippled boy laugh and clap his hands when they wheeled him outside to see the finished scene.

All this and much more pa was telling mamma while she ambled about, getting supper on the table.

Lillie came home. Lillie was the youngest of their three children and she worked for the Dillinghams, too, but in the department store. Lillie was a whiz with a needle, and a humble helper in the remodeling room. She made her own dresses at home and tried them on Maisie, the manikin. That was one of the store's moronic-looking models which had lost an arm and sundry other features, and Lillie had asked for it when she found they were going to discard it. Ernie, her brother, had brought it home in his car and repaired it. Now she hung her own skirts on Maisie to get their length. That was about all the good the manikin did her, for Lillie's circumference was fully three times that of the model.

The three of them sat down to eat, as Ernie would not arrive for a long time and mamma would warm things over for him. As usual, the table talk came largely from pa. He had to tell it all over to Lillie: the blue lights, the reindeer, the Santa-with-one-foot-in-the-chimney.

Lillie, who was a bit fed up with pasteboard reindeer and synthetic Santas at the store, thought she still would like to see them. So pa said tomorrow night after Carrie got here they would all drive to High View, that he himself would like to see them once from the paved street instead of with his head caught in an evergreen branch or getting a crick in his neck under a reindeer's belly.

They discussed the coming of the older daughter and her husband, Bert, and the two little boys, who were driving here from their home in another county and planning to stay two whole nights. A big event was Christmas this year in the Mill Street Kurtz house.

After supper when Lillie started the dishes, pa went out to see to the team and mamma followed to pick out two of her fat hens for the Christmas dinner.

In the dusk of the unusually mild December evening, mamma stood looking about her as with the eye of a stranger. Then she said she wished things had been in better shape before Carrie and Bert got here, that not one thing had been done around the place to fix it up since the last time.

"That rickety old shed, pa," she said mildly. "I remember as well as I'm standin' here you tellin' Carrie you was goin' to have that good new lumber on by the next time she come."

It was as match to pine shavings. It made pa good and mad. With him working his head off, day and night! He blew up. In anyone under 12 it would have been called a tantrum. He rushed over to the tool house and got his hammer and started to yank off a rotten board.

"I'll get this done before Carrie comes," he shouted, "if it's the last thing I do."

A psychoanalyst, after much probing, might have discovered what caused pa's sudden anger. But mamma, who knew less than nothing about psychoanalysis, having only good common sense, also knew what caused it.

Pa's own regrets over his big mistake made him irritable at times. He was one of those farmers who had turned their backs on old home places during the protracted drought. Mamma had wanted to stick it out another year, but he had said no, they would move to town where everybody earned good money. So they had sold the farm and bought this little place on Mill Street, the only section of town where one could keep a cow and chickens. The very next year crops were good again and now the man who had bought the old place for so little came to River City in a car as fine as the Dillinghams'. Yes, any casual criticism of the Mill Street place always touched him in a vital spot of his being. So he yanked and swore and jawed, more mad than ever that mamma had walked away and was not hearing him.

It was not hard to get the old boards off. Soon they lay on the ground in a scattered heap of rotting timbers. Bird and Bell, from their exposed position across the manger, snatched at the alfalfa hay, quivered their nostrils and looked disdainfully at proceedings. The cow chewed her cud in the loose-jawed way of cows and stared disinterestedly into space.

Looking at the animals of which he was so fond, pa admitted to himself he needn't have ripped the boards off until morning, but balmy weather was predicted all through Christmas. And mamma had made him pretty mad. Suddenly the fire of his anger went out, for he was remembering something Ernie had said and it tickled his fancy. The last time Carrie brought her little boys home, Ernie had told them it was bubble gum the cow was chewing and the kids had hung over the half door an hour or more waiting for the big bubble to blow out.

Tomorrow night the little kids would be here and the thought of it righted the world again.

Mamma came toward him with two hens under her arms as though she wanted him to make up with her. But he fussed around among the boards, not wanting to seem pleasant too suddenly.

His flashlight lay on the ground, highlighting the open shed, and the street light, too, shone in. An old hen flew squawking out of the hay and the pigeons swooped down from the roof.

Mamma stood looking at it for quite a while, then all at once she chucked the hens under a box and hurried into the house. When she came out, she held Maisie, the manikin, in front of her and Lillie was close behind with her arms full of sheets.

"What you think you're up to?" pa asked.

"You let me be," mamma said pointedly. "I know what I'm doin'."

She set up the manikin and with deft touches Lillie draped the sheets over its body and head and arranged it so it was leaning over the manger. Then mamma put pa's flashlight down in the manger itself and a faint light shone through the cracks of the old boards.

"There!" said mamma, stepping back. "Don't that look for all the world like the Bible story?"

"Seems like it's makin' light of it," pa said critically. "The Scotts and the Dillinghams didn't do nothin' like that. They just used Santy Clauses."

"I ain't doin' it for show, like them," mamma retorted. "I'm doin' it for Carrie's little boys. Somethin' they can see for themselves when they drive in. Somethin'

they'll never forget, like's not, as long as they live."

Mamma and Lillie went out to the fence to survey their handiwork from that point. They were standing there when Ernie drove into the yard. Ernie worked for the River City Body and Fender Wreck Company, and one viewing the car and hearing its noisy approach would have questioned whether he ever patronized his own company.

They were anxious to know what Ernie thought. There were the horses nuzzling the alfalfa, the cow chewing away placidly, and the pigeons on the ridge-pole. And there was the white-robed figure bending over the faint glow in the manger.

Ernie stood without words. Then he said "For gosh sakes! What in time?" The words were crude, but the tone was reverent.

"Mamma did it for the kids," Lillie said. "She wants you to fix a star up over the stable. Mrs. Dillingham gave an old one to pa."

Ernie had been a fixer ever since he was a little boy. Not for his looks had the River City Body and Fender Wreck Company hired Ernie Kurtz. So after his warmed-over supper he got his tools and a coil of wire and fixed the yellow bauble high over the stable, the wire and the slim rod almost invisible, so that it seemed a star hung there by itself.

All the next day pa worked up on High View Drive and all day mamma cleaned the house, made doughnuts and cookies with green sugar on them, and dressed the fat hens, stuffing them to the bursting point with onion dressing.

Almost before they knew it, Christmas Eve had arrived, and Carrie and Bert and the two little boys were driving into the yard with everyone hurrying out to greet them.

"Why, mamma," Carrie said. "That old shed . . . it just gave me a turn when we drove in."

But mamma was a bit disappointed over the little boys. The older one comprehended what it meant and was duly awe-struck, but the younger one ran over to the manger and said: "When's she goin' to blow out her bubble gum?"

After they had taken in the wrapped presents and the mince pies Carrie had baked, pa told them how they were all going to drive up to High View and see the expensive decorations, stressing his own part in their preparation so much that mamma said, "Don't brag. A few others had somethin' to do with it, you know." And Ernie sent them all into laughter when he called it High Brow Drive.

Then he went after his girl, Annie Hansen, and when they came back, surprisingly her brother was with them, which sent Lillie into a state of fluttering excitement.

So they all started out in two cars. Ernie and his girl and Lillie in Ernie's one seat, with the brother in the back, his long legs dangling out. Carrie and Bert took their little boys and mamma and pa. Not knowing the streets leading to the winding High View section, Bert stayed close behind Ernie's car, which chugged its way ahead of them like a noisy tugboat.

Everyone was hilariously happy. As for pa, his anger about mamma's chidings was long forgotten. All three of his children were home and the two little kids. The Dillinghams didn't have any children at all for Christmas fun. *We never lost a child,* he was thinking, *and the Porters lost that little girl. Our grandkids tough as tripe, and the Scotts got that crippled boy.* It gave him a light-hearted feeling of freedom from disaster. Now this nice sightseeing trip in Bert's good car. Home to coffee and doughnuts, with the kids hanging up their stockings. Tomorrow the presents and a big dinner. For fleeting moments Pa Kurtz had a warm little-boy feeling of his own toward Christmas.

Mamma, too, said she hadn't had such a good time since Tige was a pup. And when one of the little boys said he wanted to see Tige when they got back, everyone laughed immoderately.

They passed decorated houses and countless trees brightly lighted in windows. Then around the curving streets of the High View district, following Ernie's noisy lead so closely that Carrie said they were just like Mary's little lamb. Across the street from the Porters' colonial house, Ernie stopped, and they stopped too.

The evergreens with their sparkling blue lights seemed a part of an enchanted forest. Carrie said she never saw anything so pretty in her life and waxed so enthusiastic that pa reminded her again of his big part in it.

When Ernie yelled back to ask if they'd seen enough, pa waved him on. And around the curve they went to the Dillinghams'.

There were other cars in front of the houses. Pa said like as not the judges themselves were right now deciding the prizes, and by the tone of his voice one would have thought the fate of the nation hung on the decision.

At the Dillinghams', the little boys waxed more excited over the reindeer, lighted by the searchlight which threw them into snow-white relief. Yes, pa said, it was worth all the work they'd put on them.

Then to Doctor Scott's, and here the little boys practically turned inside out. For Santa himself was up on the roof as plain as day; and more, he was singing "Jingle bells, jingle bells." When he stopped, they clapped their hands and yelled up at him: "Hi, Santy! Sing more." And the adults all clapped too.

Then Ernie signaled and the little procession swung down out of High View and circled into the part of town where the blocks were prosaically rectangular and everything became smaller; yards, houses, Christmas trees.

"Look!" mamma said happily. "Ain't it nice? There ain't no patent on it. Everyone can make merry. Every little house can have its own fun and tree, just the same as the big ones."

Over the railroad tracks they went and into Mill Street, where Ernie adroitly picked his way around the mushy spots in the unpaved road, with Bert following his zigzag lead. And the trip was over.

There were Bird and Bell and the cow. There were the pigeons huddled together on the stable roof. There were the white Mary and the light in the manger, and the star. The laughter died down. Everyone got out quietly. Carrie ran her arm through her mother's. "I like yours, too, mamma," she said.

Inside, they grew merry again. Over the doughnuts and sandwiches there was a lot of talk. They argued noisily about the prize places for the decorated houses, betting one another which ones would win. Carrie and Lillie both thought the lights in the trees were by far the most artistic. Ma and Ernie's girl were for the reindeer at Dillinghams'. But Lillie's potential beau and Ernie and Bert and the little boys were all for the Scotts' Santa Claus. Pa, as one who had been the creator of them all, stayed benignly neutral.

After a while Ernie took his girl home. Her brother stood around on the porch awhile with Lillie and then left. The little boys hung up their stockings, with the grown folks teasing them, saying Santy could never find his way from the Scotts' down those winding streets.

Mamma and pa kept their own bedroom. Lillie took Carrie in with her. Bert made the little boys a bed on the old couch, with three chairs in front to keep them from falling out. She had no sheets left for them, but plenty of clean patchwork quilts.

In the morning there were the sketchy breakfast and the presents, including a dishpan for mamma, who had never had a new one since her wedding day; the bit and braces pa had wished for so long; a flowered comb-and-brush set for Lillie; and fully one-third of the things for which the little boys had wished.

The children could play with their new toys and the men pitch horseshoes, but mamma and the girls had to hop right into the big dinner, for everyone would be starved. Ernie's girl and her brother were invited, too, and when they came, said they could smell that good dressing clear out in the yard. The hens practically popped open in the pans and mamma's mashed potatoes and gravy melted in the mouth. Oh, never did anyone have a nicer Christmas than the Kurtzes down on Mill Street.

It was when they were finishing Carrie's thick mince pies that the radio news came on, and the announcement of the prizes. So they pulled back their chairs to listen, with the girls cautioning the menfolks, "Now stick to what your bet was last night and don't anybody cheat by changing."

The announcer introduced the committee head, who gave a too wordy talk about civic pride. Then the prizes:

"The third prize of ten dollars to Doctor Amos R. Scott, 1821 High View Drive." That was Santa-in-the-chimney. And while Ernie and his group groaned their disappointment that it was only third, the others laughed at them for their poor bet.

"The second—25 dollars—Mr. Ramsey E. Porter, 1484 High View Drive." The blue lights! With Carrie and Lillie wanting to know what the judges were thinking of, for Pete's sake, to give it only second, and mamma and Ernie's girl calling out jubilantly that it left only their own choice, the reindeer.

Then a strange thing happened.

"Listen, everybody."

"Sh! What's he saying?"

"The first prize . . . for its simplicity . . . for using materials at hand without expense . . . for its sacred note and the fact that it is the personification of the real Christmas story of which we sometimes lose sight . . . the first prize of 50 dollars is unanimously awarded to Mr. Harm Kurtz at 623 Mill Street."

A bomb would have torn fissures in the yard and made an unmendable shambles of the house, but it could not have been more devastating.

For a long moment they sat stunned, mouths open, but without speech coming forth, and only the little boys saying: "He said you, grandpa; he said you."

Then the hypnotic spell broke and Ernie let out a yell: "Fifty bucks, pa! Fifty bucks!"

And mamma, still dazed, kept repeating like some mournful raven, "But I just did it for the little boys."

Several got up and dashed over to the window to see again this first-prize paragon. But all they could see was bird and Bell and the cow out in their little yard, an old dilapidated shed, and high up over it a piece of yellow glass.

In the midst of the excitement pa practically turned pale. For it had come to him suddenly there was more to this than met the eye. What would the Scotts and the Porters and the Dillinghams say? Especially Mr. Dillingham, whose expensive reindeer had won no prize at all. He was embarrassed and worried. The joy had gone out of winning the prize. The joy had gone out of the day.

The girls had scarcely finished the dishes before the Mill Street neighbors started coming to have a share in the big news. The Danish Hansens came and the Russian family from the next block, all three of the Czech families down the street, and the Negro children who lived near the mill. They were all alike to mamma. "Just folks." She gave everyone a doughnut. In fact, they ate so many, that late in the afternoon she whipped up another batch. Also, out of honor to the great occasion, she combed her hair again in that high skinned-up way and put on a second clean apron. Two clean aprons in one day constituted the height of something or other.

"Somebody might come by," she said by way of apology.

"They'll get stuck in the mud if they do," said Ernie. "I'm the only one that knows them holes like a map."

Mamma was right. Somebody came by. All River City came by.

Soon after dusk, with the star lighted and Bird and Bell back in the shed, the cars began to drive past in unending parade. Traffic was as thick as it had ever been up on Main and Washington. You could hear talk and laughter and maybe strong words about the mud holes. Then in front of the yard, both the talk and the laughter would die down, and there would be only low-spoken words or silence. Bird and Bell pulling at the hay. The cow gazing moodily into space. The pigeons on the ridgepole in a long feathery group. White Mary bending over a faint glow in the manger. And overhead the star.

In silence the cars would drive away and more come to take their places.

Three of them did not drive away. They swung in closer to the fence and all the people got out and came into the yard. Of all things!

"Mamma, there come the Scotts and the Porters and the Dillinghams." Pa was too excited for words and hardly knew what he was doing.

But mamma was cool and went out to meet them. "Sh! They're just folks, too."

The Scotts were lifting the wheeled chair out of the car, which had been custom built for it. Doctor Scott wheeled the little boy up closer so he could see the animals. Carrie's little boys ran to him and with the tactlessness of children showed him how they could turn cartwheels all around his chair.

"Why, Mr. Kurtz," Mrs. Porter was saying, "you're the sly one. Helping us all the time and then copping out the prize yourself."

Pa let it go. They would just have to believe it was all his doings, but for a fleeting moment he saw himself yanking madly at the shed boards.

Mrs. Her-I-don't-like Scott said, "It's the sweetest thing I ever saw. It made me feel like crying when I saw it."

Mrs. Dillingham said it made their decorations all look cheap and shoddy by the side of the manger scene. Even Mr. Dillingham, who had won no prize, said, "Kurtz, you certainly deserve it."

Pa knew he couldn't take any more praise. At least, not with mamma standing right there. So he said, "I guess it was mamma's idea. She's always gettin' ideas."

Right then mamma had another one. "Will you all please to step inside and have a cup of coffee and a doughnut?"

The women demurred, but all the men said they certainly would.

So they crowded into the kitchen, mink coats and all, and stood about with coffee and doughnuts. And Lillie got up her courage and said to Mr. Dillingham, "I don't suppose you know me, but I work for you."

"Oh, yes, sure; sure I do," he said heartily, but Lillie

knew he was only being polite.

"And this is a friend of mine," she added with coy bravado, "Mr. Hansen."

Mr. Dillingham said, "How do you do, Mr. Hansen. Don't tell me you work for me, too."

"Yes, sir, I do," said Lillie's new beau. "Packing." And High View and Mill Street both laughed over it.

Mrs. Scott said, "Did you ever taste anything so good as these doughnuts? You couldn't find time to make me a batch once a week, could you?" So that Mrs. Dillingham and Mrs. Porter both said quickly, "Not unless she makes me one, too."

And mamma, pleased as Punch, but playing hard to catch, said maybe she could.

Mr. Porter was saying to Ernie, "You folks ought to have some gravel down here on Mill Street."

And Ernie, who wasn't afraid of anyone, not even a councilman, said with infinite sarcasm, "You're telling me?"

The big cars all drove away. Three or four others straggled by. Then no more. And pa turned off the light of the star.

The house was still again except for the adenoidal breathing of one of the little boys. Even Ernie, coming in late, stopped tromping about upstairs. Everyone had to get up early to see Bert and Carrie off and get back to work. It made pa worry over his inability to get to sleep. This had been the most exciting day in years.

Mamma was lying quietly, her heavy body sagging down her side of the bed. It took all pa's self-control to pretend sleep. Twice he heard the old kitchen clock strike another hour. He would try it.

"Mamma," he called softly.

"What?" she said instantly."

"Can't get to sleep."

"Wha's the matter?"

"Keep thinkin' of everything. All that money comin' to us. Company. Attention from so many folks. Children all home. Folks I work for all here and not a bit mad. You'd think I'd feel good. But I don't. Somethin' hangs over me. Like they'd been somebody real out there in the shed all this time; like we'd been leavin' 'em stay out when we ought to had 'em come on in. Fool notion—but keeps botherin' me."

And then mamma gave her answer. Comforting, too, just as he knew it would be. "I got the same feelin'. I guess people's been like that ever since it happened. Their conscience always hurtin' 'em a little because there wa'n't *no room for Him in the inn*."

59

The Christmas Nightingale

Eric P. Kelly

One of the most memorable Christmas stories to come out of that oft-ravaged country we call Poland is the one that relates the tale of the Nightingale, the boy whose ancestry no one knew but who could sing like the birds. He could imitate their every call, but only belatedly did he learn to converse with humans.

As this story is read by more westerners it will surely become as beloved on this continent as it is in Europe.

It was in the Forest of Lubel in the days of King Kasimir. The snow was crusty and hard beneath the hunter's foot, and the wind roared in the crowded pines. Few there were, peasants or townsfolk, who cared to venture into this forest; for wolves and other wild beasts ran there seeking their food, and no less feared were those human wolves, exiles and thieves, who sought refuge there.

Many miles from the main road, in the very center of this huge forest, there was a great clearing. One first became aware of it when the pines began to thin, and one could see a half circle of larches at the border—a tree seldom found in the whole domain of Poland. In the clearing inside the larch circle was a tiny grove of lindens, their branches bare and ragged in the frosty air. Beeches and oaks grew there also.

In front of the lindens stood a small peasant cottage, built longer ago than men remembered. All about it in the earth were deep pits, where glowed red fires from which the peasant took charcoal to supply the kitchens of Lublin and Krasnik many miles away.

Warfare between beast and beast, man and man, and man and beast, ended at the circle of larch trees surrounding the clearing. Since earliest time it had been on the books of the courts of the empire, of Bohemia, and of Poland, among the Lechs, the Rus, and the Czechs, that the place of the charcoal burner in mid-forest was a sanctuary of abiding peace. The peasant there must kill no animal, save for protection or food or clothing, under pain of death. The stag, fleeing from dogs, was safe within that circle; falcon pursuing pheasant must be recalled at the larches. Wolves becoming an annoyance to the charcoal burner or his family must be driven outside the circle if possible before being slain.

Some say that this custom grew up because of the presence of the lindens, beneath which St. Adalbert first preached Christ to the Slavs. Others say that the larch is a sacred tree, that it was once a tall woman with sharp head and round skirts who was made immortal by the witches of Lithuania. Little Elzbieta says that there is always peace beneath the lindens because Our Lord was crucified upon a linden, and never again may blood be shed beneath its branches. Practical-minded ones know that Otto of Germany instituted the decree, because his charcoal burners, living in the forests, had slain much game, thus curtailing the pleasure of the gentry who kept horses and hounds.

It was merry that night in the charcoal burner's humble hut. A great fire leaped and roared in the open fireplace, upon both sides of which hung dried vegetables in strings. The wife, busy with supper, ceased work for the moment to gaze at the happy scene. Her two sons, Michal and Pawel, were weaving a rough skein of hemp into cord; her husband was sharpening a charcoal cutter, while Elzbieta sat at his feet, engaged in childish prattle.

Although some cold crept in through the chinks in the wall and thatch, none of them seemed to notice it in the rich glow of the fire. The spirit of the blaze was such magic that it transformed everything it touched, the rough stools into kings' thrones, the pine-bough beds into fancy couches, canopied and hung with damask; the pewter became the finest silver, the wooden spoons were white ivory, and the copper kettle shone like burnished gold.

Elzbieta clapped her hands. "I wonder what will come tonight—perhaps a reindeer from the North."

"Nay, little one, the reindeer are gone these many years. They roam no more our Polish forests."

"There will be a hoot owl," offered Michal, the elder of the two boys.

"Not an owl—a kruk (raven)," said Pawel.

"Father," appealed Elzbieta, "I will have no owl or kruk. I will have my reindeer."

"Now, let the child alone," the mother admonished the boys.

"It is dark in the forest and there is much snow," went on Elzbieta, "and through it there comes some living thing to seek our hearth."

"And God preserve him, in this bitter cold," exclaimed the father.

"I hear the wind in the trees. It dies down when it reaches the larches."

"It was so when the reindeer came," answered the father, reminiscently.

"There was snow on the ground," Elzbieta went on with a much-told story.

"There was snow on the ground and the moon shone, but it was very cold," said the father.

"Except within the lindens. The wind ceased at the larch trees, and the cold at the lindens."

"And there was peace," continued the man. "Now on that night there came a reindeer from the North. He was huge and handsome, and had horns like the branches of a tree. On his forehead shone a great star."

"And on his back—" Elzbieta guided the course of the story.

"And on his back there rode a little boy as old as Elzbieta. About the boy's head there was a ring of fire, and the garments he wore were of white fur. In his right hand he carried a tiny tree which gleamed like a torch

61

in the forest. The wolves stole away in front of him, and the sables and hares came out to look, knowing that nothing would harm them while he was in sight."

"He was the Christ Child," said Elzbieta.

"Straight through the forest went the reindeer, until he came to a clearing where there was a cottage beneath the linden trees."

"It was the charcoal burner's cottage."

"He knocked at the door—"

As if the words had been taken from his lips and made real, there came at that very moment an actual knocking sound at the door. It was not the heavy blow of the knuckles that a man makes—not the continued knocking of a woman or child—but the brushing sound that an animal makes when it is fleeing for refuge toward the fire of its master.

The father sprang to the door and opened it.

"The Christ Child," screamed Elzbieta; for the figure of a boy was revealed.

They all stood for the moment motionless, until the mother, first of all to come to her senses, exclaimed: "Christ Child or no, the poor lad is nearly stiff from cold. Shut the door, Michal, and lead him to the fire."

Then they crowded about him, scarcely daring to touch his garments. He, but little aware of the stir he had created, looked up at them with the most human pair of brown eyes in the world, and tottering, exhausted from cold and hunger, fell in a faint in the good woman's arms.

She laid him gently on a bed of boughs which the boys dragged close to the fire.

"He will come to himself shortly," she gave as her opinion, after they had rubbed his limbs and done what they could for him, "and then he must drink some hot soup." So carefully straining a portion of borsch (beet soup) through a piece of cloth, she placed the bowl beside him, and regarded him.

Elzbieta, bolder than the rest, had done more than regard him. She passed her hands over his hair, which, uncaught by a cap, fell in golden ringlets about his shoulders. Then she touched a little silver ornament, a star with a white stone in the center, that hung about his neck. The velvet of his blouse which matched his knickerbockers was soft beneath her fingers. At throat and wrist were turned back the ruffled collar and cuffs of a silken shirt.

A short time passed. He stirred and moaned, and his eyes opened again.

"The Lord bless you," exclaimed the mother. "What do you call yourself, child?"

The lips moved, but no sound came from them.

She raised him then and poured the soup into his mouth. He drank clear to the bottom of the bowl, and she poured it full again.

"He is famished," she exclaimed.

He was, but in his youthful body vitality soon reasserted itself. A touch of color appeared in the cheeks. The pulse began to throb again where Elzbieta held wrist and hand. He glanced eagerly here and there about the room as if searching for something that he knew, but unable to find it turned back to little Elzbieta, and with his gaze resting on her sweet, childish face, the look of terror that had been apparent in his eyes died out in a flash and the lids fell.

"God has sent him to our sanctuary," spoke the father, softly.

He slept there before the fire while the boys went out to gather more boughs. At length when the flames began to flicker and die, Elzbieta sought her bed in the corner near her mother and father, while the two boys, scarcely daring to speak aloud, went to their rest with much nudging and whispering.

The morning brought no further enlightenment concerning the identity of the guest. He was of gentle birth—that was clear, for the skin of hands and face was white and delicate to the touch. Beyond conjecture, however, it was impossible to go, for he could not speak a word, even under the kindest of persuasions. That he understood what was said, they perceived, for he would nod or shake his head or gesture with his hands.

"Perhaps he may have been born with some affliction," said the father; "but more likely some fright in the woods has caused him to lose his power of speech."

The good pastor from the distant church upon one of his visits gave the boy much attention, but was as perplexed as they. "I have heard of no missing children in the houses of great folk hereabout, and such a one as this would have been sought for long ago. He has intelligence above the ordinary, anyone can see, and I, too, believe it was that night of wandering and terror in the woods that robbed him of his power of speech; I have seen men struck dumb by fright at lesser things." It was quite evident, though, that the memory of that dark time and what preceded it had gone from his mind, for he was now as happy as a lark.

In the course of time his coming was taken for granted. His fine clothes were laid carefully away, and one of Pawel's homespun suits was fitted to him. The only reminder of his former state remained in the silver token which still hung about his neck, though hidden from sight beneath his rough blouse.

He was then in his fifth or sixth year, perhaps, and entered readily into the outdoor life led by Michal and Pawel. The soft white hands hardened, the cheeks filled and became ruddy, his health improved daily.

For two years he never spoke a word, although the foster parents tried in many ways to coax him to it, and even attempted to teach him as they had their own children. Something in his brain was dead, or sleeping. Then late one night in summer, in the third year after his coming, the charcoal burner woke with a start from his slumber.

"Wife," he said, "wake thyself. There is a nightingale in the cottage. Someone must have left the door open."

Elzbieta had heard it, too. She was sitting up on the pine boughs trying to arouse the boys with whispering.

For, from the corner where the strange boy slept, came a song miraculously like that of the nightingale. First there was the low, sighing note which the bird breathes forth as it settles itself on a bough, and then the quaver, expectant and marvelously human, as it listens for the reply of its mate. A smooth flow of melody followed, and then there came the first notes of its inspired music before it pours forth its soul in song.

"Never was nightingale known to enter the house of human beings before," whispered the charcoal burner. "We are much blest, my wife."

The song continued. In it were all the feelings of life on earth and life to come. There was the sadness of the poets, the love of mothers for their children, the affection of fathers for their own.

"It is not a bird; it is the stranger," cried little Elzbieta, gazing at the adopted boy. "His lips are moving. I can see him in the light that falls through a chink in the thatch." At that he wakened, and the music ceased.

Nevertheless, the next day the gift was still with him. The life in the open, the humble and healthful fare, the kindness and love everywhere about him, had all begun to react upon that dark spell which had cast its shadow upon his consciousness.

By some strange prank of nature the long-dumb tongue was gifted with unusual powers. Songs of birds he could reproduce almost to perfection; calls of wild animals, the snarling of wolves, the baying of the forest dogs, the hoot of owls—with these he delighted the charcoal burner's family. Then, though poured forth at first without words, came the songs of the common folk, the melodies which the workers sang at the pits, the joyous tunes and ballads which the children sing while at play.

And from the depths of his heart came other songs that he had once heard, yet which brought no definite face or picture before him. One of these was a soft, low melody, which made one think of the pleasant dusk, the fading sunlight.

The mother shed tears over it. "It is thy dear mother's lullaby," she said as she clasped him to her breast; "canst thou not remember her?"

He struggled with his thoughts, but that black curtain, bred of terror or cruelty, hung there and he could not see behind it.

And thus it was that they called him the "Nightingale."

With the passing of years he learned to speak, groping at the beginning for words like a child seeking the meanings of things. His first word was "Elzbieta," his second "mother," and these two words he repeated over and over again, as if with pride and happiness in a beloved possession.

He was about in his twelfth year when there came the cold winter that men speak of today in the Lublin district. Frosts settled early in the fall, driving away the summer birds a few weeks earlier than usual, and by the middle of the month of Listopad or Falling Leaves (November) the ground was covered with hard-crusted snow. Huge flocks of the black birds called kruks swarmed into Poland from the steppes of Asia and south Russia; deer and wild boar crowded tamely together about the glowing charcoal pits in the forest; mighty oaks cracked asunder of nights in the hideous cold, and the river Wieprz was frozen clear to its muddy bed.

From the towns came a call for wood and charcoal.

Men and women crammed fuel into the brick stoves and open hearths, in an attempt to drive back the penetrating cold; and in such quantity did they consume this fuel that by the week before Christmas the supplies laid in for the whole winter had disappeared. At that, riders went forth from the towns, north and south, seeking for wood and charcoal, and in the forests the sound of axes and falling trees made a continual roar from morning till night. In the charcoal burner's pits an unwonted supply of wood smoked and charred throughout the day, and when dusk fell the towers of black smoke changed into vistas of red and yellow flames.

One rider, making his way over the crust, had ridden clear from Zamosc, to the south and east of Lublin, up to the charcoal burner's hut in the forest in search of fuel. The entire supply of charcoal on hand he contracted for immediately at an astoundingly high price, with the provision that a large load of it was to be delivered at once by the burner to the castle in Zamosc.

Even though it was in the dead of winter, the charcoal burner was quick to take advantage of this opportunity for a journey, with perhaps other orders when he had reached the city. Besides, he had always wished to have his children see something of the world outside the forest, and now had come the chance. Pawel he was forced to leave behind with the mother, but he took Michal and Elzbieta and the Nightingale. The father himself drove the span of oxen that drew the large sled, and Michal followed with another in which rode the children upon more sacks of charcoal.

Life on the road was in itself an enthralling and extraordinary adventure for these children. When once clear of the forest and along the highway toward the town, they joined in a great caravan of companies like their own, bound for the same destination, for the Christmas season was at hand, and money was plenty in Zamosc. There were sleighs laden with small trees for the holiday; traveling booths that would open for the sale of gifts and goodies; platform sleighs whereon players would enact scenes from the life of our Lord. There were Cossacks with little horses, upon which they could stand and dance; Tartars who could whirl for an hour without tiring, or juggle swords for pennies; and even Gypsies, who had laces and cashmeres and read one's fortune in the palm of the hand.

For five days the ox-drawn sleds creaked over the hard crusts. The days were a bit warmer than in the week preceding, but the nights were bitterly cold. It was the charcoal burner's duty as each day ended to find some humble tavern or hospitable farmhouse for his charges, where the oxen could be stabled and fed, and the children put to sleep upon the benches or floors. Wrapped in their bearskin coats and robes, they had suffered nothing from the cold; even their feet had kept warm and comfortable in their high leather boots.

Women greeted the children with joy, and gave them the choicest places in their humble huts; while between the men passed always the customary greeting, "Niech bendzie pochwalony Jesus Christ!" (May Jesus Christ be praised.)

And the reply, "Na wieki wieku." (To the Ages of Ages.)

And then they were given steaming beet soup; and when they had drunk it, there was placed before them stews of vegetables, bread, dried fish, and sometimes meat.

Toward the close of the fifth day, the sleighs stood beneath the walls of the gloomy castle of Zamosc, gloomy because it rose into the sky unlighted, overlooking the town. It was Christmas Eve, and the Star which betokens the coming of the Christ Child was already hanging like a great lamp high in the heavens. The keeper of the draw lowered the bridge and admitted them, whispering, "Jesus Christ is born," to which they replied with readiness, "May His holy name be praised."

"You are expected," said the gatekeeper, "but I warn you to make no noise while within the castle walls. The great lady orders it so each year, and all must obey."

Wondering at this, they passed in in silence. But there was gaiety in the castle yard, nevertheless. A company of boys carrying a star went by singing in a low tone, "Wsrod nocy cisy" (Through Night's Dark Shadow), and candles were gleaming from the rear of the company where some were carrying a Szopka or stable, a little box made of wood in which puppets would be made to enact the thrilling scenes of those days in Bethlehem when Christ was born.

The oxen had scarcely come to a halt before the charcoal burner leaped to the ground and hurried for the kitchen in search of the seneschal who would tell him where to stable his beasts and leave his supplies. The children, left to their own devices, began to exchange greetings with the crowd of Christmas revelers—the boys following the star, the servants of the mansion, soldiers, and porters. Elzbieta prevailed upon the Nightingale to entertain the crowd with a song, and in a moment the sound of his sweet voice in the sharp, crisp air drew all about the sleigh, and the applause made the castle walls ring.

But at that, a man in watchman's armor and carrying a lantern and spear came hurrying toward the company. "What is the meaning of all this noise here?" he demanded angrily. "Has not the lady given commands these many years that silence should be kept in this court on this night? To your homes, all of you."

"Sir"—the boy with the star stepped up before him—"I give you my word that we will make no such noise again, if you will but permit us to go about, singing our carols and showing our puppets. For you know that tonight Christ is born, and every heart in Christendom is happy."

The guard looked toward the upper windows doubtfully. "I know," he said, "but a command is a command, and it is because it was on a Christmas Eve . . . However," he debated with himself for a moment, "I will allow you to proceed, but make no noise that can be heard above. Were this clamor to come to the lady's ears—but go on." He went back to his post, gazing with a melancholy air upon the heights above the yard.

Truly they were melancholy, too. A palace with less gaiety on this joyous night one might seek for in vain in all Poland. Its grim walls and buttresses seemed to be grimmer and drearier than ever, in comparison with the lights and happiness below, and the huge turrets soaring aloft into the starlight were severe, and somber, and cheerless.

High up in the castle, in a room hung with dark tapestries, an elderly man of severe countenance was standing by a couch upon which reclined a woman. She was not old, but the suggestion of some fearful experience distracted the attention somewhat from the actual beauty of her countenance. She was dressed in a long black velvet robe caught at the waist with a golden buckle. From her throat hung down upon her breast a slender golden chain, at its end an ornament of silver—the emblem of the house of Sigismund Rey.

The man was evidently an old servitor, a legal clerk perhaps. He had been reading from a parchment which he held in his hands.

"Thus, with the death of your second brother, the property reverts entirely to you," he said. "All others who might make claim to it are now—" He was about to say "dead," but changed to "with God's holy angels."

"Little does it mean to me, Stefan. Indeed, my own days are numbered in this world."

"Not so, my lady," he answered softly. "Do you not recall what the learned doctor from Krakow said? That you were only weary and sad, and that in due time will come back to you the spirit that we love? My lady"—he bent over her—"I have served your family for many years. I drew up for your father the deeds which bequeathed the property to your brothers and you, and afterward to the first male heir, be he yours or theirs. Now be to us who love Zamosc as a mistress who loves her people. There are fearful wrongs, suffered at the hands of your brothers, to be righted, sufferings to be recompensed, hearts to be gladdened. We have had but little peace hereabouts these many years."

His appeal had but little effect. "Stefan, I tell you truly that my heart is sick of life. All that I have loved has perished. There remains to me nothing of flesh and blood that is my own. It is better that I should die. My brothers are dead. My husband died in the plague year in Poznan; and I am without kin or living issue."

Her hand rose to her throat as if the heavy air of the room were stifling her. "Throw aside the tapestries at the casement, Stefan," she commanded, "and let in the air."

He moved to the opening and drew back the cloth, and almost at the same instant a gentle burst of melody floated up from below. It came so sweetly sudden, and with such power and depth, that the man stood for a moment motionless, gazing into the court below. The lady, likewise, at the sound of it raised her head. It was the sound of the Nightingale, the song of deep woods and limpid lakes—now one bird calling to another, now the wind stirring in the tops of the pine trees, now the rain pattering on the soft needles underfoot. Then all at once the music died away like the light raindrops that vanish in the sun.

"What was that?" she demanded, staring.

"A peasant boy standing on an oxcart, my lady—" Stefan hesitated. "You know that it is Christmas Eve?"

"Do I know—when it was on Christmas Eve, so long ago, they told me that my son—"

"The boys have come with the star and Szopka."

She thought, sighed deeply, then raised herself on one arm. "Bring them up here."

Stefan went to her from the casement, an expression of wonder on his face. "But, my lady, you usually forbid them— Here, in this room?"

"Yes, they may save me from my thoughts."

He rushed to the door and called. A retainer answered, heard his words, then darted down the steps to the courtyard below.

A few minutes later he returned ushering in the company, with Elzbieta, Michal, and the Nightingale following curiously.

"Come before me," she commanded. The children fell upon their knees.

"You have the Szopka?"

"We have, my lady." Two boys rose and brought the little puppet show forward. Stefan adjusted a chair and extinguished all the candles except those which illuminated the little stage, so that nothing was perceptible save the space where the Christ Child in roughly carved wood lay sleeping, and the Madonna hovered above him. Behind the rude stall were seen the heads of cattle, and in front shepherds were kneeling.

"Begin," she commanded.

"I am Bartek, the shepherd," recited one of the boys. "It is Christmas Eve and I am sleeping on the hills."

"And we are shepherds," shouted four others.

The play proceeded. The angel comes from the sky to rouse the shepherds to make the pilgrimage to Bethlehem. They meet a soldier at the Bethlehem gate who warns them that Herod the king dislikes shepherds. Herod in his robes shouts at the top of his terrible voice when he hears that a new king is born, and orders the children of all Israel to be put to death.

At this point the first act ended, and the chorus came forward to sing.

While they were singing, the woman turned to Stefan, her eyes wet with tears. "Stefan," she murmured wistfully, "I believe that everyone in the world is happy this night except me. Would to God I had my own child in my arms and might sing him the lullaby that my mother sang to me." She gave way utterly, though quietly, to her tears.

As her mind dwelt on her old grief, however, the tears dried, and there came the burning of pain that extinguishes the moisture in the springs from which tears flow. Sweetly, sweetly, through it, came the memory of her dead boy—as the child that he was when he slept in her arms and she sang to him the lullaby that every nurse in the house of Rey had sung since the days of Krakus the king. For a moment the mere recollection of that melody soothed the fire of anguish, touching like cooling oil the throbbing courses of her thought. The accents rose at first from her heart, then intensified, until the music seemed everywhere.

Then suddenly it ceased in her thoughts, but, miracle of miracles, it passed to her actual senses—surely its joy was in the air. Her soul became passive. She drank in the loved measures as if they were food for the soul. Was it reality, or was it imagination? The music was in the air. It was too soft to echo in the distant corners of the room or to reverberate against the walls, but it was there, rising from the dark space in front of her like a priest's benediction.

"Light the candles," she cried, rising from the couch. "Who was singing that song?"

The leader of the Szopka, he who bore the star, fell upon his knees before her, and answered, "A peasant boy, my lady. He has been singing to us in the court, and we brought him with us."

The candles were lighted, and the Nightingale was hurried forward. He was about to kneel before her, wondering in his simple heart why the lady had taken such an interest in his song, when suddenly he was swept aside as by a veritable tempest, when the elderly Stefan threw himself at the woman's feet.

"Now, I must tell you"—he spoke wildly—"the secret that I expected to carry to the grave. And it were better for you that I had, since it can but add to the burden that you already bear. There is that in this scene that wrings it from me—Christmas Eve—the children—the Szopka —the lullaby of the House of Rey—My lady, your boy perished six years ago in the Forest of Lubel."

"The Forest of Lubel," she

spoke perplexedly, for it seemed to her that the man's senses had suddenly taken flight. "He died six years ago, it is true, when I was away in Poznan."

"It was when you were in Poznam," the man went on urgently, "that your brothers—traitors beyond any of your dreams—decided that your son should not stand in their way. They imprisoned the child in a secret room of this very castle, circulated word of his illness, death, and burial, and then, not quite willing to kill him with their own hands, it seemed, they planned for him a no less awful fate. He was taken by night to a distant forest, a thick forest overrun with wolves, from which not even an unarmed man, much less a child, could come forth alive.

"The man who had held the horses on the night of this expedition came to me secretly, months later, unable longer to contain the story. He said that four men had accompanied the boy, and that he had heard one of them mutter: 'I see no joy in this excursion. It is a four days' ride behind swift horses to this part of the Lubel Forest.' Another had said; 'Silence, you fool,' and they had started. The four men never returned.

"And now, my lady, punish me as you will. I knew this—that to tell you at the time, when it was too late, was the same thing as to strike you dead."

As the man had proceeded with his story he had become quieter, his words ringing truer and truer through his sincerity and grief, until the listener's face had paled. She was sobbing as he finished his tale.

And the Nightingale, still standing near, wondering, unhappy at the sight of the great lady's sorrow, placed his hand timidly upon her sleeve. At the light touch she seemed to leap from her world of sorrow to living reality, and the cadence of the lullaby burned again in her brain. "You—child!" she exclaimed. "Who are you? And where did you learn that song?"

She took the boy's face in her hands, and turned it toward the light, and as she saw his features clearly for the first time, "Stefan—Stefan—" she screamed. "Look

at this boy! Whence came he, and why has he this hair and eyes and voice? Am I growing mad—or what—"

But it was the boy who answered her somewhat bashfully. "I came with the charcoal burner from the Forest of Lubel, and I am called the Nightingale."

"From the *Forest of Lubel?*" Stefan started and came toward the boy. "How old are you?"

"I know not exactly. It is six years that I have lived in the forest."

Stefan stared at the boy and at the woman. Neither of them noticed him, for they had sensed some feeling in common and their eyes seemed to meet in some bond.

"Your father and mother—are they living?"

"That I know not. My foster father is the charcoal burner, and his wife my dear foster mother."

"But your real father and mother?"

"That I do not know."

Elzbieta pressed forward and took the boy's hand in her own. "He came to us out of the forest one evening long ago, before Christmas. Something had happened to him, for he could not speak; and indeed he did not speak for long afterward. But we call him the Nightingale, for he sings like one, and he knows the language of all the animals in the forest."

The veins stood out on Stefan's head. He stepped to the boy's side and put his fingers beneath his chin, so that he must look up into his eyes. "Think; think," he commanded. "Was it four men in a wagon who took you into the forest on that winter night? Do you not remember wolves and the cold?"

"I don't know, good sir . . . I can't think. And yet . . . wait . . . perhaps . . ." He was silent for a moment, while, at some suggestion from these words, old memories poured again into his head. "It was not a wagon, sir," he shouted suddenly. "It was a sleigh. The runners creaked on the snow—"

"God be praised," cried Stefan. "Tell us what happened next?"

Then out of the darkness of his mind, out of the cloud which had descended so long ago, a cloud of terror, which mercifully the tender mind had not been able to endure—"I remember," he continued, "the forest was full of eyes. . . ."

"Wolves," muttered Stefan.

"And the men let me go. I ran into the forest and heard them screaming behind me."

"Met their righteous fate—eaten by wolves," from Stefan.

"I ran until I saw a light streaming from beneath a door."

"Our cottage," said Elzbieta. "And he came like the Christ Child in the story."

"He is Stanislaus—my boy—" The lady's lips were unsealed. "He has come back to me from death," and she caught him up into her embrace.

"Bring the charcoal burner hither," called Stefan, and he was brought in. He told his story briefly, confirming what the children had disclosed; then, gently disengaging the boy from the woman's arms, held up before them the charm which hung about the boy's neck. It matched the lady's charm, except for size, in every particular.

And at that, the wildest shouts of joy ran through the castle. "The boy is alive." "Our own has come back to us," was shouted from man to man. They threw open the window hangings, set the place aglow with candles, and called in the musicians, who filled every corner of the castle with melody. An hour later, when all were tired of feasting, the lady sat upon her couch, no longer the saddened, disillusioned spirit that had grown tired of life, and forsworn happiness, but a transformed being, aglow with life, eyes shining, cheeks radiant.

The chorus gathered around. The leader tuned them, and they sang:

"Vivat Pan Jesus, Vivat Marya,
Vivat i Josef, sna compania."

And through it all the Nightingale sat on the couch beside his mother, one hand grasped firmly in hers, and the other held proudly by little Elzbieta.

My Christmas Miracle

Taylor Caldwell

So famous and renowned is Taylor Caldwell to us today that it is difficult for us to conceptualize her as a wan, depressed, and frightened young mother; alone, nearly destitute, jobless, and having to face the bleakest Christmas of her life. She had almost lost faith in God Himself.

And then . . .

For many of us, one Christmas stands out from all the others, the one when the meaning of the day shone clearest.

Although I did not guess it, my own "truest" Christmas began on a rainy spring day in the bleakest year of my life. Recently divorced, I was in my 20s, had no job, and was on my way downtown to go the rounds of the employment offices. I had no umbrella, for my old one had fallen apart, and I could not afford another one. I sat down in the streetcar, and there against the seat was a beautiful silk umbrella with a silver handle inlaid with gold and flecks of bright enamel. I had never seen anything so lovely.

I examined the handle and saw a name engraved among the golden scrolls. The usual procedure would have been to turn in the umbrella to the conductor, but on impulse, I decided to take it with me and find the owner myself. I got off the streetcar in a downpour and thankfully opened the umbrella to protect myself. Then I searched a telephone book for the name on the umbrella and found it. I called, and a lady answered.

Yes, she said in surprise, that was her umbrella, which her parents, now dead, had given her for a birthday present. But, she added, it had been stolen from her locker at school (she was a teacher) more than a year before. She was so excited that I forgot I was looking for a job and went directly to her small house. She took the umbrella, and her eyes filled with tears.

The teacher wanted to give me a reward, but—though $20 was all I had in the world—her happiness at retrieving this special possession was such that to have accepted money would have spoiled something. We talked for a while, and I must have given her my address. I don't remember.

The next six months were wretched. I was able to obtain only temporary employment here and there, for a small salary, though this was what they now call the Roaring Twenties. But I put aside 25 or 50 cents when I could afford it for my little girl's Christmas presents. (It took me six months to save $8.) My last job ended the day before Christmas, my $30 rent was soon due, and I had $15 to my name—which Peggy and I would need for food. She was home from her convent boarding school and was excitedly looking forward to her gifts the next day, which I had already purchased. I had

bought her a small tree, and we were going to decorate it that night.

The stormy air was full of the sound of Christmas merriment as I walked from the streetcar to my small apartment. Bells rang and children shouted in the bitter dusk of the evening, and windows were lighted and everyone was running and laughing. But there would be no Christmas for me, I knew, no gifts, no remembrance whatsoever. As I struggled through the snowdrifts, I just about reached the lowest point in my life. Unless a miracle happened I would be homeless in January, foodless, jobless. I had prayed steadily for weeks, and there had been no answer but this coldness and darkness, this harsh air, this abandonment. God and men had completely forgotten me. I felt old as death, and as lonely. What was to become of us?

I looked in my mailbox. There were only bills in it, a sheaf of them, and two white envelopes which I was sure contained more bills. I went up three dusty flights of stairs, and I cried, shivering in my thin coat. But I made myself smile so I could greet my little daughter with a pretense of happiness. She opened the door for me and threw herself in my arms, screaming joyously and demanding that we decorate the tree immediately.

73

Peggy was not yet 6 years old, and had been alone all day while I worked. She had set our kitchen table for our evening meal, proudly, and put pans out and the three cans of food which would be our dinner. For some reason, when I looked at those pans and cans, I felt brokenhearted. We would have only hamburgers for our Christmas dinner tomorrow, and gelatin. I stood in the cold little kitchen, and misery overwhelmed me. For the first time in my life, I doubted the existence of God and His mercy, and the coldness in my heart was colder than ice.

The doorbell rang, and Peggy ran fleetly to answer it, calling that it must be Santa Claus. Then I heard a man talking heartily to her and went to the door. He was a delivery man, and his arms were full of big parcels, and he was laughing at my child's frenzied joy and her dancing. "This is a mistake," I said, but he read the name on the parcels, and they were for me. When he had gone I could only stare at the boxes. Peggy and I sat on the floor and opened them. A huge doll, three times the size of the one I had bought for her. Gloves. Candy. A beautiful leather purse. Incredible! I looked for the name of the sender. It was the teacher, the address simply "California," where she had moved.

Our dinner that night was the most delicious I had ever eaten. I could only pray in myself, "Thank you, Father." I forgot I had no money for the rent and only $15 in my purse and no job. My child and I ate and laughed together in happiness. Then we decorated the little tree and marveled at it. I put Peggy to bed and set up her gifts around the tree, and a sweet peace flooded

me like a benediction. I had some hope again. I could even examine the sheaf of bills without cringing. Then I opened the two white envelopes. One contained a check for $30 from a company I had worked for briefly in the summer. It was, said a note, my "Christmas bonus." My rent!

The other envelope was an offer of a permanent position with the government—to begin two days after Christmas. I sat with the letter in my hand and the check on the table before me, and I think that was the most joyful moment of my life up to that time.

The church bells began to ring. I hurriedly looked at my child, who was sleeping blissfully, and ran down to the street. Everywhere people were walking to church to celebrate the birth of the Savior. People smiled at me and I smiled back. The storm had stopped, the sky was pure and glittering with stars.

"The Lord is born!" sang the bells to the crystal night and the laughing darkness. Someone began to sing, "Come, all ye faithful!" I joined in and sang with the strangers all about me.

I am not alone at all, I thought. *I was never alone at all.*

And that, of course, is the message of Christmas. We are never alone. Not when the night is darkest, the wind coldest, the world seemingly most indifferent. For this is still the time God chooses.

A Small Gift of Love

Mary Ellen Holmes

Nurses. Just what is it that inspires these ministering spirits to endure day after grueling day, continually interacting with human nature at its unloveliest? But, even so, there are nurses . . . and there are nurses; the latter so loving, so empathetic, so giving, so kind that they approach angelhood themselves. Of such a breed was Nurse Johnson.

No one who has ever read Mary Ellen Holmes' "Christmas Island" (Christmas in My Heart, book 2) will ever be able to forget it. This is another of her inimitable stories first published by Salvation Army's The War Cry.

The whole story of the doll reads like a fairy tale spun from gossamer, for there is mystery in it and romance, light and shadow, tears and laughter.

But if, in the end, you hear the song of angels and see a distant star, then you will know why it happened just the way it did, and why it should be told this Christmas season.

To begin with, no one really knew where the doll came from. It was just there, in its nurse's uniform, inside the door of the Salvation Army hall when the captain came back to pack Christmas baskets that bitter December day in 1918.

The war was over, but influenza was raging across the country. Captain Dunlap, who had been on volunteer duty at the hospital since early November, had begged an eight-hour leave that afternoon.

"Just long enough to get the baskets packed and delivered," she told the supervisor. "Where there is illness and unemployment there is also hunger. And there will be the children wishing for toys in the morning—and the old folks counting on the woolen socks and shawls the home league has been knitting."

"God love you!" the supervisor said—and the words were not strange on her tongue, for she had grown accustomed to them during the weeks the captain had worked on the floor with her, sharing the living and the dying. "If I could, I'd help you myself!"

It was dusk when the captain left the hospital—that time of day when the world is cloaked in a gray mist of transition between sun and stars—and she did not really see the doll until her overshoe touched it just inside the front door in the dark little hallway leading into her office. She reached down and felt, rather than saw, the smooth china of the face, the bulky softness of the nurse's cap, and the piece of paper pinned to the stiff white of the uniform apron.

Under the light on her desk she read the words. "Please give this doll to some little girl who will love it. Her name is Florence."

The note was unsigned.

And so—in the beginning—no one really did know

where the doll came from at all.

Ellen Johnson was just 8 years old when the small gift of love which was the doll was given to her. Exactly 8, for she had been born on Christmas day, and it may well be that the Christmas birthday had prompted Captain Dunlap when she placed the doll, carefully wrapped in white tissue, on top of the Johnson food basket.

Or perhaps it was just that, from the moment she picked the doll up in the darkened hallway, the captain had been thinking how excited Ellen would be over the white uniform, the starched cap, the nurse's apron. Ellen, who at 8 already knew that she *had* to be a nurse some day. Ellen, who, still almost a baby herself, could soothe a crying infant with her touch, or bring a fever down, or calm a frightened, hurt child, or bandage a wound, or heal a broken bird wing.

It was a long climb up five flights of stairs to the tiny room and a half where Ellen lived with her grandmother since her parents had been killed in a fire in a shabby tenement building across town, but to Captain Dunlap, the bushel basket grew lighter with every step. There was a small chicken in the basket, and potatoes, milk and butter, some onions and carrots, and a soup bone. There was a homemade fruitcake wrapped in Christmas tissue and a knitted, warm shoulder shawl for Granny Johnson. And on top of the basket, carefully covered with white tissue, there was the doll. It was as if Captain Dunlap carried a little of heaven and earth in her arms. And who knows, perhaps she did!

Ellen heard her coming, and rushed headlong down the last flight to meet her. "Merry Christmas, Captain!" she called from the landing. "Merry, merry Christmas!" At the child's insistence, Captain Dunlap released one wire handle of the basket toward her and together, carrying it between them as if it were a great treasure chest of gold, they climbed the fifth flight of stairs.

Inside the little apartment everything was spotless and shining. On a table near the window a lone branch of pine lent a sweet Christmas fragrance to a tiny nativity scene, carefully, skillfully fashioned from magazine cutouts and matchsticks.

Captain Ann Dunlap lived to be 69, and until the day she died she never forgot the look on Ellen Johnson's face when she first saw the doll. Mostly it was the eyes, so large and luminous to start with, so filled with childlike hope and wonder. Christmas eyes, they were—and if you have ever met anyone born on Christmas Day you will know what that means.

The captain could not remember, afterward, what was said in the little room that late Christmas Eve. But she could remember, always, the eyes—the swift delight, the incredible joy, the great gratitude, and the sudden tears that welled like jewels and dropped like silver rain.

And in that room, in that moment of time and space, the captain knew that, somehow, Ellen Johnson would be a nurse because someone, with the small gift of love which was the doll, had given her a star to follow.

A dozen swift years came and went—and in them Ellen Johnson and "Florence" became something of a legend in Manhattan. It was as if God had granted Ellen a special gift of healing. She had only to walk into a room and the sunshine came with her. She went gladly, willingly, wherever there was suffering or pain or sorrow, and always when she left there was peace and calm behind her. If the patient were a child, then Florence accompanied Ellen, and often over the years the doll was left, clasped tightly in a child's arms, until a crisis passed, or a broken leg healed, or a rheumatic heart grew strong.

When finally, at 20, Ellen was able to enter nurse's training, she was already more a nurse than many nurses ever learn to be. When she was capped she stayed on in the hospital and, although she was often offered promotions, she preferred to be what she was—a floor nurse, with a special affinity for those who needed her most. Somehow the most irascible patients accepted her, the most critically ill rallied, the most unhappy found hope.

And so it was not unusual at all that Ellen should have taken a special interest in Mrs. Jonathan Brewster from the moment she entered the hospital, for Mrs. Brewster was all three problems in one—irascible, critically ill following a heart attack, and utterly (and volubly) unhappy.

During his lifetime, Mr. Brewster had donated generously to the hospital, and his will had left a bequest large enough to build a children's wing in memory of the little girl the Brewsters had lost many years before. Now, in her illness, Mrs. Brewster reverted often to the past, one moment haughtily demanding service, the next pitifully crooning a lullaby to an imaginary child she rocked endlessly in her arms. Vestiges of grace and beauty still clung to her body, but bitterness and selfishness so overshadowed her spirit that in the first week of her hospitalization she went through eight private-duty nurses, dismissing all of them and finally deciding not to hire any more.

Dr. Brock, who attended her, was more than a little troubled, but even he could not persuade her to treat her nurses as if they were human beings. It was almost as if Mrs. Brewster hated nurses and deliberately wanted them to hate her.

The family physician who turned the case over to Dr. Brock had been stricken himself with a heart attack two days after admitting Mrs. Brewster. From his own hospital bed, he had given explicit instructions and a grave warning, "She's like a dowager without a dynasty," he advised. "All her life she's had her own way and, difficult though it will be, you'll have to appease her in every way you can. To antagonize or upset her in her present condition would be fatal."

There were many times, in the weeks which followed, when Dr. Brock wondered if it would not be fatal for him if he continued to "take" Mrs. Brewster. In the old days, he might have been able to talk out his frustration with his wife, but Dr. Brock had been a widower for three years, and so he worried only his own heart with the old lady he wanted so desperately to help.

Through it all, though, Ellen Johnson was a godsend. Not that Mrs. Brewster was any less harsh with Ellen than with the others. If anything, she was even more critical and demanding. But in spite of it—or perhaps because of it—Ellen quietly came more often than necessary to the room, ministering to Mrs. Brewster's needs, speaking gently, making her comfortable.

As Christmas approached, Ellen tried several times to share with Mrs. Brewster the plans and preparations being made in the hospital for the holiday. But Mrs. Brewster would have none of it. At the mention of Christmas she became sullen and melancholy and one day, when Ellen was especially happy over decorating the tree in the children's ward, Mrs. Brewster lashed almost violently. "Christmas is stupid and senseless, and so are all the people who believe in it," she declared, staring icily at Ellen.

"Never that, Mrs. Brewster," Ellen answered as gently as if she were placating a disobedient child. "Christmas is full of warmth and wisdom. The very thought of the birth of the Christ Child makes me glad inside."

"Humbug!" Mrs. Brewster snorted, and if she had learned the word from Scrooge himself she could not have delivered it more convincingly. "If there is a God He would know better than to try to save the world with a baby."

"It was the only way He could," Ellen said. "If Jesus had come to earth as a king, people might have followed Him because of His power, or His wealth. When God sent Him as a tiny baby lying in a manger He knew that people would come to Him only because they loved Him. That's what Christmas really is, Mrs. Brewster—a small gift of love to lead men back to God."

"Love!" Mrs. Brewster rejoined. "Was it love that took away my only child?"

"Love gave her to you in the beginning," Ellen said softly, "and death does not really take away, except for just a little while."

They did not speak again of Christmas until Sunday afternoon, and then it was Dr. Brock who was responsible for the incident.

Sunday was Ellen's usual day off, but she had stopped by the hospital anyway just to see how Mrs. Brewster was. And so she was there, in the room, when Dr. Brock brought the Christmas tree.

It was a small artificial tree on a tiny stand, gaily decorated with old-fashioned ornaments and golden tinsel. He placed it carefully on the bedside table and smiled at Ellen across the glimmering star crowning the top branch.

"Merry Christmas to both of you," he said gaily. "I haven't had a Christmas tree since my wife died, and I decided I wanted to share it with my favorite patient."

"Get it out of here!"

The words were sharp, hysterical. "Get it out of here, I said." Mrs. Brewster raised up from the pillow, her face flushed, her mouth distorted, her breathing harsh and irregular.

In a moment Ellen had lifted the tree from the table, carried it into the corridor and rushed back to help Dr. Brock with his patient. It took a long time to calm Mrs. Brewster but finally, when she had dropped into an uneasy sleep, Ellen followed the doctor into the hall. He stood there awkwardly, holding the tree, looking like a small boy who had been punished for something he could not understand.

"She doesn't really mean to be unkind," Ellen said. "It's just that she's old and lonely and afraid."

The doctor looked at Ellen, her beginning-to-gray hair under the little hat reaching almost but not quite to her shoulder, and before the gentle understanding in her eyes he was suddenly ashamed and shy.

"You're right," he said. "She really is!" And then, mostly because he wanted to express the warm glow he felt stirring within him at that moment, he handed Ellen the tree. "The tree isn't much," he said, "but the ornaments were mine when I was small, and the star is one my father made."

Love comes in many different ways, but never more simply or never more beautifully than it came that Sunday before Christmas to Ellen Johnson and Dr. David Brock, standing in the hospital corridor outside the door of an irascible old woman who had been their Cupid.

The days following that Sunday were filled with work and wonder. Ellen was more nurse than ever now, for love lent a new magic to her touch; and her happiness was a golden cup, full and running over, to be shared by all her patients.

All, that is, except Mrs. Brewster, who grew daily more irritable and hard to please. She was sitting up a little bit at a time now, berating everyone in the hospital, especially Ellen. But when the supervisor sent Ellen to the other end of the hallway on emergency duty, Mrs. Brewster demanded her back immediately. "She's the only one around here I can stand to look at," she said.

Finally, Christmas Eve came.

In the rest of the hospital there was the same hustle and bustle which accompanies Christmas any place. In the kitchen the turkeys were ready for their special stuffing; in the wards the Christmas trees were trimmed; from the hospital windows candles sent gleams across the snow; and in the corridors the carolers sang of a silent night, of a manger in Bethlehem, and of three kings bearing gifts and following a star.

But Mrs. Brewster would have none of it at all.

She asked the night nurse to close the transom, and when the carolers stopped at her door to wish her a merry Christmas she ordered them, imperiously, away.

She was sitting up in bed when Ellen knocked softly at the door and entered, carrying the tissue-wrapped package. It was late, for there had been—as there always are—many Christmas Eve emergencies. Ellen was tired, and the tiredness showed in her eyes, but she had felt compelled all day to do what she now did.

"Merry Christmas, Mrs. Brewster," she said brightly. "I've brought you a gift."

"I have no need for gifts!"

Suddenly, Mrs. Brewster turned her face away from Ellen's look of compassion. "Merry Christmas, indeed. To me, this is only the day my daughter died." And then, as if she needed to be superior to cover up the tremor in her voice, she added icily, "What gift could you possibly give to me that would be of any value?"

"It's the greatest gift I have to give," Ellen said simply, "and I don't really know why I want you to have it, but I do."

Awkwardly, she placed the box on the bed and started for the door.

"Wait!" The word was sharp and demanding, and Ellen answered the command as naturally as she would have obeyed a doctor's order. "Take the gift with you," Mrs. Brewster said. "I don't need it."

"Oh, but you do!" And suddenly all the things Ellen had wanted to say for so long were pouring out in a torrent of words—kind words, beautiful words, words touched with tenderness and tolerance.

"It's more than a gift I bring you in the box," Ellen said. "It's all the things that gift meant to me. I was 8 years old when someone sent it to me for Christmas. My parents were dead, and I was sometimes hungry, and always poor, and often afraid. But somehow, after that Christmas I was never really any of those things again. It was as if this were more than a gift—it was a symbol. Someone had shared love with me and kindness. Someone had sent hope to me wrapped in white tissue paper. Someone had given me a star in the darkness of my despair."

"And now . . ." the whispered words came strangely from Mrs. Brewster's lips, ". . . and now I am poor and hungry and afraid. And all my money cannot bring me love or hope—and nowhere in the darkness can I see a star—"

"The star is there," Ellen said, "and if only you will let us, David and I will love you. That's why I brought the gift to you, to tell you now—as it told me then—that you are not forgotten."

Carefully she unwrapped the tissue from the box and placed the doll in its white uniform in Mrs. Brewster's cradled, empty arms.

For a long moment there was silence in the room, and then suddenly Ellen saw in Mrs. Brewster's eyes the same unforgettable things Captain Dunlap had seen in hers so many years before—the swift delight, the incredible joy, the great gratitude, and the sudden tears welling like jewels and dropping like silver rain.

Even before she heard the words, Ellen knew—it was as if she had known from the first moment Mrs. Brewster entered the hospital . . .

"It's Florence!" Mrs. Brewster said slowly, unbelievingly. "It's the Christmas doll I bought so many years ago for my little girl. It's the doll I took to the Salvation Army hall the afternoon my daughter died in the flu epidemic in 1918."

And so, in the end—as it was in the beginning—the story of the doll reads like a fairy tale woven from gossamer. There is mystery in it and romance, light and shadow, tears and laughter.

But most important of all, there is in it, and running through it, the great glorious message of Christmas itself—that no kindness is ever lost, and that a small gift of love is still the world's greatest miracle.

Yet Not One of Them Shall Fall

Hartley F. Dailey

Why is it that we value human life but fail to respect the non-human counterpart? We recoil in horror from a person who murders a human being but laud the marksmanship and manual dexterity of the person who slaughters animals and birds just for the sport of it. Does our Lord really care what happens to these smaller creatures? "Yes," observed the apostle Matthew. Hartley Dailey, author of "The Red Mittens" (one of the most cherished stories in Christmas in My Heart, book 1), explores this concept in this poignant narrative. Even though this story is not included in the Four Gospels, Dailey felt it would be in character for it to have actually happened, especially in light of the apostle John's concluding words:

> *But there are also many other things which Jesus did; were every one of them to be written, I suppose that the world itself could not contain the books that would be written (John 21:25).*

All day the sky had hung leaden and threatening over the "City of David," the sleepy little town of Bethlehem. It was the time of the rains, but no rain was falling; neither rain nor snow had thus far blessed

the fields and groves round about. The countryside lay parched and dry, shivering beneath an unnatural northeast wind which should not be blowing at this season at all.

Travelers poured into the town in unwonted numbers, for it was the time of the great census, when every man was ordered to journey to the place of his tribe to be counted. Camels, donkeys, oxen, and the tramp of human feet had ground the dry soil of the streets into dust. It lay ankle deep in the streets, it powdered the garments of travelers, it choked the throats and stung the eyes. It crept through the carefully shuttered windows of the houses, and lay like a pall on the furnishings within.

Here and there through the streets a group of ruffian boys wandered, six or seven untidy, unmannerly fellows, the despair alike of their parents and the village elders. Lazy, impudent, and self-willed, they seldom worked, they stayed away from school, they hung about all day on the streets causing trouble, making disrespectful remarks about passersby—in short, being generally obnoxious. Their ringleader was one Benjamin, son of Jonas, the prize miscreant of the lot, a rough ungainly lad of some 14 summers. His father, a man of considerable consequence in the town, tried in vain to control his unruly son.

Today, Benjamin had proposed a game. Each boy bore a sling, two leather thongs with a pouch between, and a bag of small round stones. As they went along the street, one would pick out a target, and challenge some other of the group to hit it. This might be something small and difficult to hit, or again, it might be something considered very daring, as a bronze kettle hanging in the stall of Jonah, the merchant, or a fancy white donkey belonging to some rich caravan owner.

Suddenly, one in the group called out, "Look there, Benjamin, across the street, on the corner of old Eli's house. Bet you can't hit that from here!"

Contemptuously, the young ruffian fitted a stone in his sling. He sneered as he drew back his arm. "Ha," he boasted, "by the beard of Abraham, I don't even need both eyes to sling at that! I could hit such a mark with one eye closed!" Expertly, he swung the sling three times around his head, and let fly the stone.

His boast wasn't idle. The stone sped straight and true, and though the little sparrow he had aimed at started to fly, it was too late. The stone struck it upon the wing. Its intended flight turned into a helpless flutter, and it went spinning down into the alley between the houses. The boys didn't even bother to go look at it, or end its misery with a merciful death. They cheered their leader and slapped his back, then, noting the approach of Eli, who was no friend of theirs, drifted away in search of other mischief.

But the bird was not without a friend: Simon, the little hunchback orphan boy, was searching up and down the alleys, hoping to find a scrap of food, or a useful bit of rag to add to his pitiful clothing. He didn't dare show himself to the other boys. His ugly misshapen form made him the butt of their jokes—and worse. His arms, as a result of his infirmity, were so weak he was incapable of defending himself. But as the miscreants moved away, he crept to the mouth of the alley, and gathered the sparrow up in his hands.

At first it struggled wildly. Simon could feel the terrified beating of its timid heart, as his hands gently stroked it, smoothing the injured wing against its side, doing his best to put the broken bone in place. Gradually, its struggles subsided till finally it snuggled down between his warming hands with a contented little chirp. Then Simon made a place for it in the bosom of the filthy rag he called his cloak, and went on with his search.

Life was hard. Disfigured from birth, he was shunned by most of the village because of his repulsive looks. Many actively hated him, for one in his condition was supposed to bring some kind of bad luck. More often than not when he asked for alms, he received blows and curses instead. He had never seen his father. When his mother died, two years ago, he had lost his last friend. The very condition which made it impossible for him to earn a living, turned away those who might have helped him.

As evening came on, he made his way toward the caravanserai at the edge of town. The cook at the inn there was a rough, hard-handed man with a heart of gold. Sometimes, if there was no one to interfere, he would allow Simon to turn the roasting spit. Later, he would give the boy scraps of food left by the guests. Comforts were few in Simon's life.

To sit in the glow of heat from the charcoal cooking fire, to smell the delicious odors of the roasting meat, these were the finest experiences he knew, and the scraps of bone and fat discarded by the guests at the inn were his most nourishing food.

But tonight was not his lucky night. Some great Roman was stopping at the inn, and he had sent his slave to the kitchen to oversee the preparation of his food. When that worthy caught sight of Simon he flew into a rage.

"Out, out, you misbegotten swine!" he shouted. "No filthy offal such as you shall hang around the kitchen where my master's food is cooked. Get out, before I throw your filthy carcass to the dogs!"

Disconsolate, Simon turned away. But the rough old cook, pretending to hurry him out, slipped a hard chunk of bread into his hand. Once outside, the boy sat down in the stable yard to eat his bread. Since he had tasted hardly a bite of food all day, even the hard dry bread tasted good. But, hungry as he was, he broke off a portion and fed it to the bird, crumb by crumb.

Later, he made his way to the stable built into the hillside behind the inn. Here were stabled the cow and donkey belonging to the innkeeper, as well as the mounts of a few more affluent travelers. Here also, in a little stall at one end, were kept a few fat sheep, waiting to be slaughtered for the inn table. Simon had often slept among them. They were gentle beasts, and their soft, woolly sides were a fine bulwark against the chill of the night; soon, his head resting on the side of one of them, he was fast asleep.

Late in the night, he was awakened by a commotion such as he had seldom heard before. A long time he lay very still, terrified that the sounds might be made by robbers attacking the caravan outside, and the attempts of the owners to drive them off. But at last, within the very stable walls, he heard the plaintive cry of a small baby. Simon could contain himself no longer: he rose to his knees, and peered between the vertical bars which separated the sheep pen from the rest of the stable. He gazed in amazement on the scene there, then rubbed his eyes to see if he were dreaming.

Seated upon a robe atop a pile of hay, a Mother held an obviously newborn baby in her lap. Gathered before her in attitudes of worship were a group of shepherds—but, more remarkable, three richly clad strangers were kneeling right there upon the dirty stable floor, and presenting costly gifts to this baby; this baby who could not have been more than a couple of hours old.

The boy watched in awe. Never had he seen such men as these, even in this town astride the caravan route from the East. And to find them here, kneeling in the stable dirt! A strange feeling crept over him. Who was this child, that these rich men should bow before him, and give him gold and other precious things? For some unexplainable reason, he wished that he might do the same.

Almost without willing it, Simon had climbed the stable bars. He thoroughly expected to be driven from the stable with blows and curses. But a roughly dressed man—he must have been the baby's father—took his hand, then led him toward the Child; and the rich men moved aside to let him pass, as though he had been a very prince. So presently he found himself kneeling there, in the forefront of all those gathered before the babe.

"My Lord," he stammered, "Dear little Baby, I too would give thee a gift. But I am only an orphan and a cripple. The only thing I have to give is the little bird I found today." He took the sparrow tenderly from inside his cloak, and held it out before him.

The mother turned the Child so that He faced Simon, and the baby suddenly opened His eyes, so that His gaze seemed to rest squarely upon the wounded bird. The sparrow seemed to shudder, and then suddenly it spread its wings, one of which had certainly been broken only a moment before, and soared into the air. Three times it circled over the heads of the transfixed watchers, then briefly hovered above the mother and Child.

Simon knelt there trembling in nervous fear and awe. Then he saw that the strange dark eyes were looking at him. Without knowing why, he felt compelled to return that gaze. He felt as if he were drowning, or falling into the bottomless pit of that fathomless gaze. There was a feeling of fiery force which seemed to flow throughout his body, then he felt turned and twisted in some way he could not understand. There was a moment of almost unbearable pain, and then he was rising to his feet.

For a moment Simon could not understand what had happened: things looked so different! It came to him that never before had he looked upon the world from this height, or from this angle. His arms had never seemed so straight, nor felt so strong. And the man who had led him in was kneeling on the floor praying, his eyes lifted Heavenward.

"Hear, O Israel," he prayed, "the Lord thy God, He is one God. Praise to Thee, O Lord, for this night have I seen Thy work begun!" Suddenly, realization came to the boy. He no longer was a hunchback.

The father of the Child came suddenly to lay a hand upon his head. "My son," he said, "tonight you have been given a new back. Such miracles are not wasted. I do not know how, but someday, when this Babe has become a man, He will have need of that back. When that time comes, though you have roamed to the very end of the earth, you will be there beside Him. By what name are you called, and whence came you?

"I am Simon, sir," the lad replied, "an orphan. My father was the leader of a mighty caravan. But he was killed by robbers in the year that I was born. He used to live in Cyrene, before he came here and met my mother. I think that I shall go there, now that I am whole and strong. Perhaps some of my father's people are living there still."

So saying, he turned away, and went out into the first light of morning.

(In the Gospel according to Matthew, we read these words of our Lord: "Are not two sparrows sold for a farthing? Yet not one of them shall fall to the ground unless your Father wills it" Matt. 10:29.)

The Story of the Other Wise Man

Henry Van Dyke

One can count on the fingers of one hand the great Christmas stories. "The Other Wise Man" is one of them.

It was born on the eve of the social-gospel movement in America; born of the realization that the Jesus of the Gospels did not spend much time talking about what we call "doctrines," but He was very concerned with how we treat one another. His entire earthly ministry could be summed up in two words: "loving service."

Stories that change the world—how do they come to be? Half a century earlier, Charles Dickens had created the genre of Christmas story with his timeless "A Christmas Carol." Nothing of comparable power had been written since.

For the 40-year-old scholar-cleric Henry Van Dyke, 1892 had been a dark and tragic year, during which his beloved father had died. The world saw merely the facade: Van Dyke at his peak—a graduate of Princeton, Princeton Theological School, and the University of Berlin; pastor of the New York's prestigious Brick Presbyterian Church; author of such scholarly work as The Poetry of Tennyson. Yet inside, he was anything but confident:

The year had been full of sickness and sorrow. Every day brought trouble. Every night was tormented with pain. They are very long—those nights when one lies awake, and hears the laboring heart pumping wearily at its task, and watches for the morning, not knowing whether it will ever dawn . . .

And the heaviest burden?

You must face the thought that your work in the world may be almost ended, but you know that it is not nearly finished. You have not solved the problems that perplexed you. You have not reached the goal that you aimed at. You have not accomplished the great task that you set for yourself. You are still on the way; and perhaps your journey must end now—nowhere— in the dark.

Well, it was in one of these long, lonely nights that this story came to me. I have studied and loved the curious tales of the Three Wise Men of the East as they are told in the GOLDEN LEGEND of Jacobus de Voragine and other medieval books. But of the Fourth Wise Man I had never heard until that night. Then I saw him distinctly, moving through the shadows in a little circle of light. His countenance was so clear as the memory of my father's face as I saw it for the last time a few months before. The narrative of his journeyings and trials and disappointments ran without a break. Even certain sentences came to me complete and unforgettable, clear-cut like a cameo. All that I had to do was to follow Artaban, step by step, as the tale went on, from the beginning to the end of his pilgrimage.

Responding to the oft-asked question: why he made the Fourth Wise Man tell a lie, to save the life of a little child, he countered,

Is a lie ever justifiable? Perhaps not. But may it not sometimes seem inevitable? And if it were a sin, might a man not confess it, and be pardoned for it more easily than for the greater sin of spiritual selfishness, or indifference, or the betrayal of innocent blood? That is what I saw Artaban do. That is what I heard him say. All through his life he was trying to do the best that he could. It was not perfect. But there are some kinds of failure that are better than success.

It is probable that more research went into this than any other Christmas story ever written. All his previous research, it appears in retrospect, had been setting the stage for this work. And now, it was not enough merely to tell the story he felt a Higher Power wished him to chronicle: it must have historical authenticity as well. So he scoured the great libraries of the world seeking information about every aspect of ancient life and travel. Not until he was satisfied that he knew his ground as well as an attorney presenting his first case before the Supreme Court did he finally begin writing.

What Van Dyke created was a story so simply and beautifully told that the reader is unaware that this recreation of the world our Lord knew is undergirded by prodigious research. It is an awesome tour de force.

On Christmas Day, 1892, he spread out his manuscript on his pulpit, looked out at the vast hushed and expectant audience, and wondered how the Fourth Wise Man's story would be received. He needn't have worried: the little story spread like wildfire. Three years later, Harpers, the most prestigious publishing house in the world, launched it out across all the seas of the world, both in English and in many translations.

In Van Dyke's original, there is a long prologue titled "The Sign in the Sky," in which the princely Artaban summons his father and his closest confidants to an urgent meeting. I am excerpting only key passages here to provide the story's setting:

He stood by the doorway to greet his guests—a tall, dark man of about 40 years, with brilliant eyes set near together under his broad brow, and firm lines graven around his fine, thin lips; the brow of a dreamer and the mouth of a soldier, a man of sensitive feeling but inflexible will—one of those who, in whatever age they may live, are born for inward conflict and a life of quest.

His robe was of pure white wool, thrown over a tunic of silk; and a white, pointed cap, with long lapels at the sides, rested on his flowing black hair. It was the dress of the ancient priesthood of the Magi, called the fire-worshippers.

Artaban's nine guests were clothed in rich attire of many-colored silks, crowned with massive golden collars around their necks (a symbol of Parthian nobility); on their chests were the winged circles of gold that identified them as *followers of Zoroaster.*

His voice taut with excitement, he shared with them the research he and his three fellow Magians, Caspar, Melchior, and Balthasar, had conducted; how the great Daniel (a prince in the two world empires, the Babylonian and their own, the Medo-Persian) had predicted the coming of "the Anointed One, the Prince," at the end of "seven and threescore and two weeks." According to their calculations, that time had now come. Furthermore,

We have studied the sky, and in the spring of the year we saw two of the greatest stars draw near together in the sign of the Fish, which is the house of the Hebrew. We also saw a new star there, which shown for one night and then vanished. Now again the two great planets are meeting. This night is their conjunction. My three brothers are watching at the ancient Temple of the Seven Spheres, at Borsippa, in Babylonia, and I am watching here. If the star shines again, they will wait ten days for me at the temple, and then we will set out together for Jerusalem, to see and worship the promised one who shall be born King of Israel. I believe the sign will come. I have made ready for the journey. I have sold my house and my possessions, and bought these three jewels—a sapphire, a ruby, and a pearl—to carry as tribute to the King. And I ask you to go with me on the pilgrimage.

While he was speaking he thrust his hand into the inmost fold of his girdle and drew out three gems—one blue as a fragment night sky, one red-

der than a ray of sunrise, and one as pure as the peak of a snow mountain at twilight—and laid them on the outspread linen scrolls before him.

But his friends remained unconvinced; led by the persuasive arguments of Tigranes, each of the others, under one pretext or another, refused to make such a sacrifice.

One by one they went out of the azure chamber with the silver stars, and Artaban was left in solitude.

In the cool of that evening, Artaban ascended to his roof terrace and searched for the sign:

Far over the eastern plain a white mist stretched like a lake. But where the distant peak of Zagros serrated the western horizon the sky was clear. Jupiter and Saturn rolled together like drops of lambent flame about to blend in one.

As Artaban watched them, behold, an azure spark was born out of the darkness beneath, rounding itself with purple splendors to a crimson sphere, and spiring upward through rays of saffron and orange into a point of white radiance. Tiny and infinitely remote, yet perfect in every part, it pulsated in the enormous vault as if the three jewels in the Magian's breast had mingled and had been transformed into a living heart of light.

He bowed his head. He covered his brow with his hands. "It is the sign," he said. "The King is coming, and I will go to meet him."

And now, the remainder of Van Dyke's story, verbatim:

By the Waters of Babylon

All night long Vasda, the swiftest of Artaban's horses, had been waiting saddled and bridled, in her stall, pawing the ground impatiently, and shaking her bit as if she shared the eagerness of her master's purpose, though she knew not its meaning.

Before the birds had fully roused to their strong, high, joyful chant of morning song, before the white mist had begun to lift lazily from the plain, the other wise man was in the saddle, riding swiftly along the high-road, which skirted the base of Mount Orontes, westward.

How close, how intimate is the comradeship between a man and his favorite horse on a long journey. It is a silent, comprehensive friendship, an intercourse beyond the need of words.

They drink at the same wayside springs, and sleep under the same guardian stars. They are conscious together of the subduing spell of nightfall and the quickening joy of daybreak. The master shares his evening meal with his hungry companion, and feels the soft, moist lips caressing the palm of his hand as they close over the morsel of bread. In the gray dawn he is roused from his bivouac by the gentle stir of a warm, sweet breath over his sleeping face, and looks up into the eyes of his faithful fellow-traveler, ready and waiting for the toil of the day. Surely, unless he is a pagan and an unbeliever, by whatever name he calls upon his God, he will thank Him for this voiceless sympathy, this dumb affection, and his morning prayer will embrace a double blessing—God bless us both, and keep our feet from falling and our souls from death!

And then, through the keen morning air, the swift hoofs beat their spirited music along the road, keeping time to the pulsing of two hearts that are moved with the same eager desire—to conquer space, to devour the distance, to attain the goal of the journey.

Artaban must indeed ride wisely and well if he would keep the appointed hour with the other Magi; for the route was a 150 parasangs, and 15 was the utmost that he could travel in a day. But he knew Vasda's strength and pushed forward without anxiety, making the fixed distance every day, though he must travel late into the night, and in the morning long before sunrise.

He passed long the brown slopes of Mount Orontes, furrowed by the rocky courses of a hundred torrents.

He crossed the level plains of the Nisæans, where the famous herds of horses, feeding in the wide pastures, tossed their heads at Vasda's approach, and galloped away with a thunder of many hoofs, and flocks of wild birds arose suddenly from the swampy meadows, wheeling in great circles with a shining flutter of innumerable wings and shrill cries of surprise.

He traversed the fertile fields of Concabar, where the dust from the threshing-floors filled the air with a golden mist, half hiding the huge temple of Astarte with its 400 pillars.

At Baghistan, among the rich gardens watered by

89

fountains from the rock, he looked up at the mountain thrusting its immense rugged brow out over the road, and saw the figure of King Darius trampling upon his fallen foes, and the proud list of his wars and conquests graven high upon the face of the eternal cliff.

Over many a cold and desolate pass, crawling painfully across the wind-swept shoulders of the hills; down many a black mountain-gorge, where the river roared and raced before him like a savage guide; across many a smiling vale, with terraces of yellow limestone full of vines and fruit trees; through the oak groves of Carine and the dark Gates of Zagros, walled in by precipices; into the ancient city of Chala, where the people of Samaria had been kept in captivity long ago; and out again by the mighty portal, riven through the encircling hills, where he saw the image of the High Priest of the Magi sculptured on the wall of rock, with hand uplifted as if to bless the centuries of pilgrims; past the entrance of the narrow defile, filled from end to end with orchards of peaches and figs, through which the river Gyndes foamed down to meet him; over the broad rice-fields, where the autumnal vapors spread their deathly mists; following along the course of the river, under tremulous shadows of poplar and tamarind, among the lower hills; and out upon the flat plain, where the road ran straight as an arrow through the stubble-fields and parched meadows; past the city of Ctesiphon, where the Parthian emperors reigned and the vast metropolis of Seleucia which Alexander built; across the swirling floods of Tigris and the many channels of Euphrates, flowing yellow through the corn-lands—Artaban pressed onward until he arrived at nightfall of the tenth day, beneath the shattered walls of populous Babylon.

Vasda was almost spent, and he would have gladly turned into the city to find rest and refreshment for himself and for her. But he knew that it was three hours' journey yet to the Temple of the Seven Spheres, and he must reach the place by midnight if he would find his comrades waiting. So he did not halt, but rode steadily across the stubble-fields.

A grove of date-palms made an island gloom in the pale yellow sea. As she passed into the shadow Vasda slackened her pace, and begun to pick her way more carefully.

Near the farther end of the darkness an access of caution seemed to fall upon her. She scented some danger or difficulty; it was not in her heart to fly from it—only to be prepared for it, and to meet it wisely, as a good horse should do. The grove was close and silent as the tomb; not a leaf rustled, not a bird sang.

She felt her steps before her delicately, carrying her head low, and sighing now and then with apprehension. At last she gave a quick breath of anxiety and dismay, and stood stock-still, quivering in every muscle, before a dark object in the shadow of the last palm tree.

Artaban dismounted. The dim starlight revealed the form of a man lying across the road. His humble dress and the outline of his haggard face showed that he was probably one of the poor Hebrew exiles who still dwelt in great numbers in the vicinity. His pallid skin, dry and yellow as parchment, bore the mark of the deadly fever which ravaged through the marsh-lands in autumn. The chill of death was in his lean hand, and as Artaban released it the arm fell back inertly upon the motionless breast.

He turned away with a thought of pity, consigning the body to that strange burial which the Magians deemed most fitting—the funeral of the desert, from which the kites and vultures rise on dark wings, and the beasts of prey slink furtively away, leaving only a heap of white bones in the sand.

But, as he turned, a long, faint, ghostly sigh came from the man's lips. The brown, bony fingers closed convulsively on the hem of the Magian's robe and held him fast.

Artaban's heart leaped to his throat, not with fear, but with a dumb resentment at the importunity of this blind delay.

How could he stay here in the darkness to minister to a dying stranger? What claim had this unknown fragment of human life upon his compassion or his service? If he lingered but for an hour he could hardly reach Borsippa at the appointed time. His companions would think he had given up the journey. They would go without him. He would lose his quest.

But if he went on now, the man would surely die. If he stayed, life might be restored. His spirit throbbed and fluttered with the urgency of the crisis. Should he risk the great reward of his divine faith for the sake of a single deed of human love? Should he turn aside, if only for the moment, from the follow-ing of a star, to give a cup of cold water to a poor, perishing Hebrew?

"God of truth and purity," he prayed, "direct me in the holy path, the way of wisdom which Thou only knowest."

Then he turned back to the sick man. Loosening the grasp of his hand, he carried him to a little mound at the foot of the palm-tree.

He unbound the thick folds of the turban and opened the garment above the sunken breast. He brought water from one of the small canals near by, and moistened the sufferer's brow and mouth. He mingled a draught of one of those simple but potent remedies which he carried always in his girdle—for the Magians were physicians as well as astrologers—and poured it slowly between the colorless lips. Hour after hour he labored as only a skillful healer of disease can do; and at last the man's strength returned; he sat up and looked about him.

"Who art thou?" he said in the rude dialect of the country, "and why hast thou sought me here to bring back my life?"

"I am Artaban the Magian, of the city of Ecbatana, and I am going to Jerusalem in search of one who is born King of the Jews, a great Prince and Deliverer of all men. I dare not delay any longer upon my journey, for the caravan that has waited for me may depart without me. But see, here is all that I have left of bread and wine, and here is a potion of healing herbs. When thy strength is restored thou canst find the dwellings of the Hebrews among the houses of Babylon."

The Jew raised his trembling hand solemnly to

heaven.

"Now may the God of Abraham and Isaac and Jacob bless and prosper the journey of the merciful, and bring him in peace to his desired haven. But stay; I have nothing to give thee in return—only this: that I can tell thee where the Messiah must be sought. For our prophets have said that he should be born not in Jerusalem, but in Bethlehem of Judah. May the Lord bring thee in safety to that place, because thou hast had pity upon the sick."

It was already long past midnight. Artaban rode in haste, and Vasda, restored by the brief rest, ran eagerly through the silent plain and swam the channels of the river. She put forth the remnant of her strength, and fled over the ground like a gazelle.

But the first beam of the sun sent her shadow before her as she entered upon the final stadium of the journey, and the eyes of Artaban, anxiously scanning the great mound of Nimrod and the Temple of the Seven Spheres, could discern no trace of his friends.

The many-colored terraces of black and orange and red and yellow and green and blue and white, shattered by the convulsions of nature, and crumbling under the repeated blows of human violence, still glittered like a ruined rainbow in the morning light.

Artaban rode swiftly around the hill. He dismounted and climbed to the highest terrace, looking out toward the west.

The huge desolation of the marshes stretched away to the horizon and the border of the desert. Bitterns stood by the stagnant pools and jackals skulked through the low bushes; but there was no sign of the caravan of the wise men, far or near.

At the edge of the terrace he saw a little cairn of broken bricks, and under them a piece of parchment. He caught it up and read: "We have waited past the midnight, and can delay no longer. We go to find the King. Follow us across the desert."

Artaban sat down upon the ground and covered his head in despair.

"How can I cross the desert," said he, "with no food and with a spent horse? I must return to Babylon, sell my sapphire, and buy a train of camels, and provision for the journey. I may never overtake my friends. Only God the merciful knows whether I shall not lose sight of the King because I tarried to show mercy."

For the Sake of a Little Child

There was a silence in the Hall of Dreams, where I was listening to the story of the Other Wise Man, and through this silence I saw, but very dimly, his figure passing over the dreary undulations of the desert, high upon the back of his camel, rocking steadily onward like a ship over the waves.

The land of death spread its cruel net around him. The stony wastes bore no fruit but briers and thorns. The dark ledges of rock thrust themselves above the surface here and there, like the bones of perished monsters. Arid and inhospitable mountain ranges rose before him, furrowed with dry channels of ancient torrents, white and ghastly as scars on the face of nature. Shifting hills of treacherous sand were heaped like tombs along the horizon. By day, the fierce heat pressed its intolerable burden on the quivering air; and no living creature moved on the dumb, swooning earth, but tiny jerboas scuttling through the parched bushes, or lizards vanishing in the clefts of the rock. By night the jackals prowled and barked in the distance, and the lion made the black ravines echo with his hollow roaring, while a bitter blighting chill followed the fever of the day. Through heat and cold, the Magian moved steadily onward.

Then I saw the gardens and orchards of Damascus, watered by streams of Abana and Pharpar with their sloping swards inlaid with bloom, and their thickets of myrrh and roses. I saw also the long, snowy ridge of Hermon, and the dark groves of cedars, and the valley of the Jordan, and the blue waters of the Lake of Galilee, and the fertile plain of Esdraelon, and the hills of Ephraim, and the highlands of Judah. Through all these I followed the figure of Artaban moving steadily onward, until he arrived at Bethlehem. And it was the third day after the three wise men had come to that place and had found Mary and Joseph, with the young child, Jesus, and had laid their gifts of gold and frankincense and myrrh at his feet.

Then the other wise man drew near, weary, but full of hope, bearing his ruby and his pearl to offer to the King.

"For now at last," he said, "I shall surely find him, though it be alone, and later than my brethren. This is

the place which the Hebrew exile told me that the prophets had spoken, and here I shall behold the rising of the great light. But I must inquire about the visit of my brethren, and to what house the star directed them, and to whom they presented their tribute."

The streets of the village seemed to be deserted, and Artaban wondered whether the men had all gone up to the hill-pastures to bring down their sheep. From the open door of a low stone cottage he heard the sound of a woman's voice singing softly. He entered and found a young mother hushing her baby to rest. She told him of the strangers from the far East who had appeared in the village three days ago, and how they said that a star had guided them to the place where Joseph of Nazareth was lodging with his wife and her newborn child, and how they had paid reverence to the child and given him many rich gifts.

"But the travelers disappeared again," she continued, "as suddenly as they had come. We were afraid at the strangeness of their visit. We could not understand it. The man of Nazareth took the babe and his mother and fled away that same night secretly, and it was whispered that they were going far away to Egypt. Ever since, there has been a spell upon the village; something evil hangs over it. They say that the Roman soldiers are coming to Jerusalem to force a new tax from us, and the men have driven the flocks and herds far back among the hills, and hidden themselves to escape it."

Artaban listened to her gentle, timid speech, and the child in her arms looked up in his face and smiled, stretching out its rosy hands to grasp at the winged circle of gold on his breast. His heart warmed to the touch. It seemed like a greeting of love and trust to one who had journeyed long in loneliness and perplexity, fighting with his own doubts and fears, and following a light that was veiled in clouds.

"Might not this child have been the promised Prince?" he asked within himself, as he touched its soft cheek. "Kings have been born ere now in lowlier houses than this, and the favorite of the stars may rise even from a cottage. But it has not seemed good to the God of wisdom to reward my search so soon and so easily. The one whom I seek has gone before me; and now I must follow the King to Egypt."

The young mother laid the babe in its cradle, and rose to minister to the wants of the strange guest that fate had brought into her house. She set food before him, the plain fare of peasants, but willingly offered, and therefore full of refreshment for the soul as well as for the body. Artaban accepted it gratefully; and, as he ate, the child fell into a happy slumber, and murmured sweetly in its dreams, and a great peace filled the room.

But suddenly there came the noise of a wild confusion and uproar in the streets of the village, a shrieking and wailing of women's voices, a clangor of brazen trumpets and a clashing of swords, and a desperate cry: "The soldiers! The soldiers of Herod! They are killing our children."

The young mother's face grew white with terror. She clasped her child to her bosom, and crouched motionless in the darkest corner of the room, covering him with the folds of her robe, lest he should wake and cry.

But Artaban went quickly and stood in the doorway of the house. His broad shoulders filled the portal from side to side, and the peak of his white cap all but touched the lintel.

The soldiers came hurrying down the street with bloody hands and dripping swords. At the sight of the stranger in his imposing dress they hesitated with surprise. The captain of the band approached the threshold to thrust him aside. But Artaban did not stir. His face was as calm as though he were watching the stars, and in his eyes there burned that steady radiance before which even the half-tamed hunting leopard shrinks and the fierce bloodhound pauses in his leap. He held the soldier silently for an instant, and then said in a low voice:

"I am all alone in this place, and I am waiting to give this jewel to the prudent captain who will leave me in peace."

He showed the ruby, glistening in the hollow of his hand like a great drop of blood.

The captain was amazed at the splendor of the gem. The pupils of his eyes expanded with desire, and the hard lines of greed wrinkled around his lips. He stretched out his hand and took the ruby.

"March on!" he cried to his men, "there is no child here. The house is still."

The clamor and the clang of arms passed down the street as the headlong fury of the chase sweeps by the secret covert where the trembling deer is hidden. Artaban reentered the cottage. He turned his face to the east and prayed:

"God of truth, forgive my sin! I have said the thing that is not, to save the life of a child. And two of my gifts are gone. I have spent for man that which was meant for God. Shall I ever be worthy to see the face of the King?"

But the voice of the woman, weeping for joy in the shadow behind him, said very gently:

"Because thou hast saved the life of my little one, may the Lord bless thee and keep thee; the Lord make His face to shine upon thee and be gracious unto thee; the Lord lift up His countenance upon thee and give thee peace."

In the Hidden Way of Sorrow

Then again there was silence in the Hall of Dreams, deeper and more mysterious than the first interval, and I understood that the years of Artaban were flowing very swiftly under the stillness of that clinging fog, and I caught only a glimpse, here and there, of the river of his life shining through the shadows that concealed its course.

I saw him moving among the throngs of men in populous Egypt, seeking everywhere for traces of the household that had come down from Bethlehem, and finding them under the spreading sycamore trees of Heliopolis, and beneath the walls of the Roman fortress of New Babylon beside the Nile—traces so faint and dim that they vanished before him continually, as footprints on the river-sand glisten for a moment with moisture and then disappear.

I saw him again at the foot of the pyramids, which lifted their sharp points into the intense saffron glow of the sunset sky, changeless monuments of the perishable glory and the imperishable hope of man. He looked up into the vast countenance of the crouching Sphinx, and vainly tried to read the meaning of the calm eyes and smiling mouth. Was it, indeed, the mockery of all effort and all aspiration, as Tigranes had said—the cruel jest of a riddle that has no answer, a search that never can succeed? Or was there a touch of pity and encouragement in that inscrutable smile—a promise that even the defeated should attain a victory, and the disappointed should discover a prize, and the ignorant should be made wise, and the blind should see, and the wandering should come into the haven at last?

I saw him again in an obscure house of Alexandria, taking counsel with a Hebrew rabbi. The venerable man, bending over the rolls of parchment on which the prophecies of Israel were written, read aloud the pathetic words which foretold the sufferings of the promised Messiah—the despised and rejected of men, the man of sorrows and the acquaintance of grief.

"And remember, my son," said he, fixing his deep-set eyes upon the face of Artaban, "the King whom you are seeking is not to be found in a palace, nor among the rich and powerful. If the light of the world and the glory of Israel had been appointed to come with the greatness of earthly splendor, it must have appeared long ago. For no son of Abraham will ever again rival the power which Joseph had in the palaces of Egypt, or the magnificence of Solomon throned between the lions in Jerusalem. But the light for which the world is waiting is a new light, the glory that shall rise out of patient and triumphant suffering. And the kingdom which is to be established forever is a new kingdom, the royalty of perfect and unconquerable love.

"I do not know how this shall come to pass, nor how the turbulent kings and peoples of earth shall be brought to acknowledge the Messiah and pay homage to Him. But this I know. Those who seek Him will do well to look among the poor and the lowly, the sorrowful and the oppressed."

So I saw the Other Wise Man again and again, traveling from place to place, and searching among the people of the dispersion, with whom the little family from Bethlehem might, perhaps, have found refuge. He passed through countries where famine lay heavy upon the land and the poor were crying for bread. He made his dwelling in the plague-stricken cities where the sick were languishing in the bitter companionship of helpless misery. He visited the oppressed and the afflicted in the gloom of subterranean prisons, and the crowded wretchedness of slave markets, and the weary toil of galley-ships. In all this populous and intricate world of anguish, though he found none to worship, he found many to help. He fed the hungry, and clothed the naked, and healed the sick, and comforted the captive; and his years went by more swiftly than the weaver's shuttle that flashes back and forth through the loom while the web grows and the invisible pattern is completed.

It seemed almost as if he had forgotten his quest. But once I saw him for a moment as he stood alone at sunrise, waiting at the gate of a Roman prison. He had taken from a secret resting-place in his bosom the pearl, the last of his jewels. As he looked at it, a mellower lustre, a soft and iridescent light, full of shifting gleams of azure and rose, trembled upon its surface. It seemed to have absorbed some reflection of the colors of the lost sapphire and ruby. So the profound, secret purpose of a noble life draws into itself the memories of past joy and past sorrow. All that has helped it, all that has hindered it, is transfused by a subtle magic into its very essence. It becomes more luminous and precious the longer it is carried close to the warmth of the beating heart.

Then, at last, while I was thinking of this pearl, and of its meaning, I heard the end of the story of the Other Wise Man.

A Pearl of Great Price

Three-and-thirty years of the life of Artaban had passed away, and he was still a pilgrim, and a seeker after light. His hair, once darker than the cliffs of Zagros, was now as the wintry snow that covered them. His eyes, that once flashed like flames of fire, were dull as embers smoldering among the ashes.

Worn and weary and ready to die, but still looking for the King, he had come for the last time to Jerusalem. He had often visited the holy city before, and had searched through all its lanes and crowded hovels and black prisons without finding any trace of the family of Nazarenes who had fled from Bethlehem long ago. But now it seemed as he if he must make one more effort, and something whispered in his heart that, at last, he might succeed.

It was the season of the Passover. The city was thronged with strangers. The children of Israel, scattered in far lands all over the world, had returned to the Temple for the great feast, and there had been a confusion of tongues in the narrow streets for many days.

But on this day there was a singular agitation visible in the multitude. The sky was veiled with a portentous gloom, and currents of excitement seemed to flash through the crowd like the thrill which shakes the forest on the eve of a storm. A secret tide was sweeping them all one way. The clatter of sandals, and the soft, thick sound of thousands of bare feet shuffling over the stones, flowed unceasingly along the street that leads to the Damascus gate.

Artaban joined company with a group of people from his own country, Parthian Jews who had come up to keep the Passover, and inquired of them the cause of the tumult, and where they were going.

"We are going," they answered, "to the place called Golgotha, outside the city walls, where there is to be an execution. Have you not heard what has happened? Two famous robbers are to be crucified, and with them another, called Jesus of Nazareth, a man who has done many wonderful works among the people, so that they love him greatly. But the priests and elders have said that he must die, because he gave himself out to be the

Son of God. And Pilate has sent him to the cross because he said that he was the 'King of Jews.'"

How strangely these familiar words fell upon the tired heart of Artaban! They had led him for a lifetime over land and sea. And now they came to him darkly and mysteriously like a message of despair. The King had arisen, but He had been denied and cast out. He was about to perish. Perhaps He was already dying. Could it be the same who had been born in Bethlehem 33 years ago, at whose birth the star had appeared in heaven, and of whose coming the prophets had spoken?

Artaban's heart beat unsteadily with that troubled, doubtful apprehension which is the excitement of old age. But he said within himself: "The ways of God are stranger than the thoughts of men, and it may be that I shall find the King, at last, in the hands of His enemies, and shall come in time to offer my pearl for his ransom before he dies."

So the old man followed the multitude with slow and painful steps toward the Damascus gate of the city. Just beyond the entrance of the guardhouse a troop of Macedonian soldiers came down the street, dragging a young girl with torn dress and dishevelled hair. As the Magian paused to look at her with compassion, she broke suddenly from the hands of her tormentors and threw herself at his feet, clasping him around the knees. She had seen his white cap and the winged circle on his breast.

"Have pity on me," she cried, "and save me, for the sake of the God of purity! I also am a daughter of the true religion which is taught by the Magi. My father was a merchant of Parthia, but he is dead, and I am seized for his debts to be sold as a slave. Save me from worse than death."

Artaban trembled.

It was the old conflict in his soul, which had come to him in the palm-grove of Babylon and in the cottage at Bethlehem—the conflict between the expectation of faith and the impulse of love. Twice the gift which he had consecrated to the worship of religion had been drawn from his hand to the service of humanity. This was the third trial, the ultimate probation, the final and irrevocable choice.

Was it his great opportunity or his last temptation? He could not tell. One thing only was clear in the darkness of his mind—it was inevitable. And does not the inevitable come from God?

He took the pearl from his bosom. Never had it seemed so luminous, so radiant, so full of tender living luster. He laid it in the hand of the slave.

"This is thy ransom, daughter! It is the last of my treasures which I kept for the King."

While he spoke the darkness of the sky thickened, and shuddering tremors ran through the earth, heaving convulsively like the breast of one who struggles with mighty grief.

The walls of the house rocked to and fro. Stones were loosened and crashed into the street. Dust clouds filled the air. The soldiers fled in terror, reeling like drunken men. But Artaban and the girl whom he had ransomed crouched helpless beneath the wall of the Praetorium.

What had he to fear? What had he to live for? He

had given away the last remnant of his tribute for the King. He had parted with the last hope of finding Him. The quest was over, and it had failed. But even in that thought, accepted and embraced, there was peace. It was not resignation. It was not submission. It was something more profound and searching. He knew that all was well, because he had done the best that he could, from day to day. He had been true to the light that had been given to him.

He had looked for more. And if he had not found it, if failure was all that came out of his life, doubtless that was the best that was possible. He had not seen the revelation of "life everlasting, incorruptible and immortal." But he knew that even if he could live his earthly life over again, it could not be otherwise than it had been.

One more lingering pulsation of the earthquake quivered the ground. A heavy tile, shaken from the roof, fell and struck the old man on the temple. He lay breathless and pale, with his gray head resting on the young girl's shoulder, and blood trickling from the wound. As she bent over him, fearing that he was dead, there came a voice through the twilight, very small and still, like music sounding from a distance, in which the notes are clear but the words are lost. The girl turned to see if someone had spoken from the window above them, but she saw no one.

Then the old man's lips began to move, as if in answer, and she heard him say in the Parthian tongue:

"Not so, my Lord: For when saw I Thee an hungered and fed Thee? Or thirsty, and gave Thee drink? When saw I Thee a stranger, and took Thee in? Or naked, and clothed Thee? When saw I Thee sick or in prison, and came unto Thee? Three-and-thirty years have I looked for Thee; but I have never seen Thy face, nor ministered to Thee, my King."

He ceased, and the sweet voice came again. And again the maid heard it, very faintly and far away. But now it seemed as though she understood the words:

"Verily I say unto thee, Inasmuch as thou hast done it unto one of the least of these My brethren, thou hast done it unto Me."

A calm radiance of wonder and joy lighted the pale face of Artaban like the first ray of dawn on a snowy mountain-peak. One long, last breath of relief exhaled gently from his lips.

His journey was ended. His treasures were accepted. The Other Wise Man had found the King.

Lonely Tree

Margaret Sangster

Loneliness . . . it's all around us, invading every crevice of our sad land—far more so than was true when this story was written earlier in this century.

There was a lonely, joyless executive, a lonely growing-old-before-her-time stenographer, and a lonely little crippled boy—and then came Christmas.

It is a joy to me to begin bringing back some of Margaret Sangster's great stories. A new generation of readers has fallen in love with her "The Littlest Orphan and the Christ Baby" in Christmas in My Heart, *book 2. In one-on-one competition, "Lonely Tree" wouldn't yield an inch to its predecessor. And if you cried before . . .*

There was a pleasant bustle about the long office, a sense of subdued hilarity, of intense eagerness, of dreams coming true. Pretty girls covered their typewriters with ungainly, black oilcloth coats; other pretty girls covered their noses with white powder jackets. And all about them surged the little waves of their excited exclamations.

"I'm going home—home," said one girl, "on the two o'clock from Grand Central. It'll be snowing when I get off the train at six—I know it'll be snowing. And pa'll meet me with the cutter . . ." Her voice was lost in the hum of general conversation.

The tall, thin woman who was head stenographer was talking. There was even a gentle note in her stark voice. "It was kind of nice," she said slowly, "of him"—her head jerked in the direction of the office with the gilt lettering on its plate glass door—"it was kind of nice of him to give us this half-day. It's our busy season now, and he might of—"

The little blonde interrupted. "Fat chance he'd 'a 'ad to make me work this afternoon!" she scoffed. "Fat chance! I got all my shopping ter do. I haven't bought so much as a button! Say, ain't it 12 yet?"

The Lonely Girl, one of the crowd but scarcely a part of it, raised tired eyes from her notebook. So the little blonde hadn't done her shopping yet. And one of the others was going home. And the rest . . . She closed the notebook suddenly; the dots and dashes had begun to blur. It seemed strange that there could be people who had no reason to buy presents, no home to go to. It seemed strange . . .

The plateglass door with its gilt lettering was swinging open, and the hum of conversation died suddenly away. Not that the man who stood in the doorway was a stern man or an unfair one—not that he frightened his employees into a respectful silence. Only—there was something so curiously aloof about him, something so impersonal, so detached. Almost like something frozen, the Lonely Girl thought, as she noted for the thousandth time his steely, blue eyes, and his straight, mirthless mouth, and the sprinkling of gray at his temples. Even his voice was like ice; there was an unwilling chill to it.

"I hope," he was saying, "that you'll have a delightful Christmas, every one of you!" Even the warmth of the wish did not quite take the coldness from his voice.

The head stenographer spoke hurriedly. "I'm sure," she said, "that we wish you the same, Mr. Hildreth. And we want to thank you for what we found this morning in our pay envelopes. It was very generous of you."

There, in the doorway, the man seemed to falter. One might almost have suspected him of being embarrassed. Yet why should the giving of extra money at holiday time prove an embarrassment?

"Oh, that's all right, Miss Jamison," he said bruskly. And then, "Merry Christmas!"

"Merry Christmas!" chorused the girls as the plate-glass door swung to behind him. Only one of them had anything further to say.

"I wonder," she said, "if he's like that with the men—the salesmen and the department heads. So far off, I mean?"

One by one they drifted out, like children released from school, each of them with her plans. Only the Lonely Girl, her lips pressed tight together, dawdled at her desk. Only the Lonely Girl, her dark eyes misty with the ache of things, lingered over the washing of her slim hands, the adjusting of her hat. When at last she closed the door of the long room behind her, it was almost one o'clock—almost an hour since the others had left.

With feet that had no need to hurry she went toward the elevator. It did not help to see that the elevator man wore a sprig of holly pinned to the lapel of his coat. Even his cheery greeting did not help. It only emphasized her aloneness—and Christmas time should never be an alone time! She murmured a common place answer to his greeting and hurried, rather blindly, toward the street.

The street—and Christmas in the air! Despite the gray sky with the hint of snow in it, despite a dampness in the wind, the Lonely Girl felt the surge of it, the veiled sting. For even as a latent happiness began to grow in her soul, the emptiness of the season—when one hasn't a family—filled her eyes with sudden tears. A stout man with a box that could hold nothing but a doll, a faded woman whose arm was braceleted with wreaths, a group of chattering schoolgirls—all of them belonged to Christmas crowds that pressed by. All of them were going somewhere—and to someone. But she was not going anywhere in particular. Or to anyone. Sharply she swung into the crowd; let it carry her along like a chip upon an ocean. For nearly a block she let it carry her, and then she saw the white restaurant with the glass front.

Perhaps it was because the cook in the window was so round and red that she paused; perhaps because the pancakes he turned had such a golden brown color. Perhaps she hesitated because it was luncheon time, and because being alone does not ease the pangs of hunger. At any rate, she paused.

"I believe," she told herself with a sigh, "I believe I'll go in and have some food. I might as well eat here as anywhere. I might as well—"

From somewhere beside her came a voice, a cheery little voice with a lilt of a reed pipe in it. "Say," said the voice, "don't he turn 'em pretty? Wouldn't you like if you could make some? An' eat a big plate of 'em, after?"

The Lonely Girl looked swiftly away from the red cook. With wide eyes she glanced down at the owner of the voice. She glanced quite far down, for the voice was fastened to a little boy, a very little boy. He, too, was alone, of all the street. The Lonely Girl, seeing the smile in his dark eyes—eyes set staunchly in a wee, white face—answered.

"Yes," she said, "I would like to make some. And eat some, too."

The child moved nearer to her with a curiously shuffling movement. It was then that the Lonely Girl noticed, with a sudden stifled cry of pity, the pathetic little crutch that he held under his arm and the cruel twist to his small back. But there was nothing pathetic or cruel about his cheery, piping voice.

"Onct," he told the Lonely Girl, "onct I had pancakes. They was grand. Onct—"

The Lonely Girl was interrupting. "Where," she questioned almost bruskly, to hide the quiver in her voice, "where is your mother, dear? What are you doing here on the street, and all by yourself?"

The child answered slowly. Somehow the lilting note in his voice was blurred, quite as if the reed had been crushed. "I ain't got any mother," he said, "nor father, neither. Mrs. Casey takes care o' me. But it ain't—" quite evidently he was quoting, "like as if I was *her own!*"

Quickly the Lonely Girl changed the subject, almost too quickly. "Do you suppose Mrs. Casey would mind very much," she questioned, "if I should take you into the restaurant with me? Then we could have pancakes together."

The face the little boy lifted to hers was alight with a sudden, incredulous joy. "Honest, do y' want *me?*" he questioned.

The girl nodded. "Honest, I do want you!" she said.

Together they went through the swinging doors, the girl and the little crippled boy. Together they took their seats opposite each other at a shiny porcelain-topped table. And together they smiled over the spotlessness of it when the order, an order that had to do with many things besides pancakes, had been given.

All about them shoppers with laden arms were hurrying in and out. There was a festive note about them. It was a curiously warming note that caught even at the heart of the little boy.

"Are you goin' t' have a tree," he questioned abruptly, "a tree an' a Santa Claus? Are you?"

The Lonely Girl answered slowly. "I'm afraid not," she told him. "Grownup people don't have trees."

The child was looking at her with a sudden ache in his great eyes. "Little boys do," he told her. And then, "*Some* little boys!" he amended.

There was silence for a moment, a silence fraught with many meanings. It was the Lonely Girl who broke it.

"It would be nice," she said, and it was as if someone else spoke through her, "it would be nice if the two of us could have a tree—and a Santa Claus—together. Wouldn't it?"

The griddle cakes and the other things had arrived. But the little boy, being just a bit different from other little boys, did not, at once, begin to eat. "It would be awful nice," he said. "It would be just awful nice. You an' me an' a tree an'—Santa Claus. Only—how'd we be sure t' get Santa Claus t' come? He never come before t' see me—not 'at I can remember!"

Almost desperately the Lonely Girl found herself wishing that she had a brother or a father, someone who would submit to the mock dignity of a white beard and a pillow-stuffed red coat. All at once she began to realize that the plans she had suggested by way of making conversation were becoming almost unbearably real.

"Let's eat our luncheon," she said softly, "and then—"

It was at that moment that, for the second time in an hour, a voice interrupted her. Such a familiar voice it was that the Lonely Girl gazed incredulously up from her plate; such a masculine voice that she dropped a heavy fork with a small clatter upon the marble-topped table. For the voice was one that she had heard perhaps a thousand times. And it was speaking with a curious anxiety in its cool tone.

"Perhaps I can help convince Santa Claus," it said. "Perhaps I can jog his memory!"

The little boy was smiling, friendly-wise, at this helpful stranger. But the Lonely Girl had risen in her place.

"Why, Mr. Hildreth," she gasped, "Mr. Hildreth! How did you happen—"

The man answered. "I saw you with the kiddie, outside," he told her. "I—forgive me—I listened to your conversation. And then I followed you in. And kept on listening. I'm a solitary man, Miss Carleton"—it was the Lonely Girl's name—"and what you were talking about touched a hidden spring somewhere in my heart. Can't we manage somehow to give the little chap a party? Can't we?"

As if in a dream the Lonely Girl heard herself answering. "I live in a small apartment uptown," she said. "We could have a tree there."

The little boy, his cheeks bulging with griddle

cakes, interrupted. "D' you mean it?" his reed voice questioned. *You ain't kidding me?*

It was the man who answered. "No, we're not kidding you," he said. And then, "I live alone, myself, Miss Carleton. I have no kin. Christmas is a rather desperate time for a man with no kin. If we three can get together—" he hesitated. "Well, it won't do any harm! And it may help us all tremendously."

"But," the question came unwillingly to the girl's lips, "but what would they think at the office—if they knew?"

All at once the man's eyes were boyishly appealing. One almost forgot the frost-like gray at his temples. "I don't give a hang for what they'd think!" he said. "Do you?"

"No, I don't," murmured the Lonely Girl.

For a moment she was near to forgetting the little boy.

* * * * *

After luncheon—an unbelievably jolly luncheon—they left the white restaurant and went out again to the street. Strangely enough, it had ceased to be a torment, that street. Or else it was that they had ceased to be apart from it—maybe it was because they had become, in some curious fashion—related to it! As the Lonely Girl helped the little boy into a certain big car drawn up to the curb, she felt like Cinderella. And as the man took his place at the steering wheel and started to weave his way through the traffic, the little boy had almost the same sort of feeling.

"It's like magic, ain't it?" said the little boy.

First of all they found Mrs. Casey in a tenement room with little air and less light. A 10-dollar bill made Mrs. Casey happy and more than reconciled to parting, for a day, with the little boy.

"A crippled kid," she said bluntly, "is a pest. I'd 'a put him in an orphanage, only his mother was my second cousin, an' I give her a promise that he'd always have a good home. Nobody'd want to adopt a cripple—not when th' 'sylums is full of healthy kids. Not—" speaking as one who gives credit where it is due, "not that Benny ain't a good boy. He is that. But he ain't much use."

With quick tears in her eyes the Lonely Girl hurried the little boy from the room. The man—who had once seemed frozen—came more slowly behind them. Perhaps there were tears in his eyes, too. But his voice was cheery, and his touch was very tender as he lifted the child again into the car.

"Where to, now?" he questioned.

The Lonely Girl spoke. "Suppose we go after our tree," she said. *"Our tree!"*

* * * * *

Again through the streets they whirled—the streets, with Christmas in the very fabric of them. The little boy sat silently, with wide eyes, and one hand clasped in the Lonely Girl's hand. And the Lonely Girl was silent, too. Only the man was not silent; he was whistling, softly and contentedly, half to himself.

In front of the largest florist shop they stopped—it was to be no cheap affair, this tree! They stopped, and the man lifted the little boy down. And they went together into the place of fragrance and growing things.

It might have been an enchanted forest that they went into, this largest florist shop, on the day before Christmas. Orchids and roses and lilies-of-the-valley! Violets, in great April clusters, and lilacs mistily sweet. Poinsettias, fairly shouting the joy of the season, and mistletoe. And back of everything the trees, spicily fragrant and thrillingly green. Back of everything—the trees!

Of course, the man wanted the largest tree. He had always wanted the best—and he had usually been able to get it; that was why his name was printed in letters of gold upon the door of a private office. He spoke authoritatively to a clerk, while the girl nodded dreamily in the background and the little boy—almost red-cheeked with eagerness—hopped up and down on his crutch. And then began the work of selection.

They touched the trees gently. This one was larger than the others—yes. But this one was almost feathery with needles, and its branches were unbelievably regular. The man and the girl, almost breathlessly eager, followed the clerk, and the little boy poked into the dimmest corners. It was his voice, suddenly, that made them pause in the work of choosing.

"I like this one," said the little boy, his wee face peering gnome-like from between two branches. "This one!"

After all, Christmas trees were for children. In nearly shame-faced manner the man and the girl turned toward the little boy.

"Which one, dear?" questioned the girl.

There was something affectionate in the way that the child's hand rested upon the twisted trunk of the smallest tree. There was a spirit of brotherhood in the touch of his thin fingers that made one notice acutely the tree's aching deficiencies. For it was a stunted tree, a bent tree, a tree that through some pitiful freak of nature had grown crooked.

There was annoyance in the clerk's voice as he spoke. "That tree," he told the man, quite ignoring the little boy, "was sent to us by mistake. It was never meant for a Christmas tree! We can only sell the best here. The very best."

For one moment the man hesitated; it was such a mean sort of broken thing. And then he turned appealingly to the girl.

"Why," he questioned, "has he chosen *that?*" A jerk of his thumb indicated the tree that had been sent by mistake.

The girl did not answer, but her heart was shining from her eyes as she went toward the little boy. She was near to understanding.

"Are you sure, dear," she questioned, "that you like that tree best?"

The little boy's voice was positive, quite positive. His cheeks were still red. "It's a cripple tree," he told the girl. "It ain't like—th' other trees. Nobody'd want it—ever—but us. It'd just get left, always. An' never trimmed with tinsel an' lights, like th' rest o' the trees 'll be trimmed. I guess it's pretty lonely for a tree that's crooked, when all th' rest of th' trees are straight!"

Even the clerk had no further objection to offer.

* * * * *

They took the tree home to the girl's apartment. On the way to the apartment they paused at sundry thrilling stores for silver ornaments and gold ones, and tiny electric bulbs in the shape of singing birds. Crepe paper they bought, and garlands of ground pine, and a huge knot of mistletoe. The motor car was like Santa's own sleigh when it stopped, finally, at its destination.

As they went up the three flights to her rooms, the man going first with the little boy upon his broad shoulders, the Lonely Girl experienced a curious feeling of unreality. She found herself wondering, suddenly, what the head stenographer would think if she could glance in, for a moment, upon their ascending backs.

As she fitted her key into a lock, she wondered what the blonde girl would say. But strangely enough, as the door swung open, it was of the girl who had talked of going home that she thought. Suddenly she was remembering how the word "home" had hurt, a few hours before. And all at once she was conscious that the word had stopped hurting. For the apartment was no longer an empty shell of a place to her. It was something brighter and better now. A child's laugh had worked the miracle; a man's step in her tiny living room had done magic things!

They propped the little boy up against cushions on the shabby sofa—not that they expected him to stay there. And then, after several trips down the three flights, they were ready.

Against a background of Christmas greens they set up the little twisted tree. It didn't look quite so crooked against the friendliness of that background. The girl's hand, slipping along one of the bent branches, brushed, quite by accident, against the man's hand. And they both smiled, almost shyly.

The little boy was exuberant. You see, it was his party! With wide eyes that held no shadow of wistfulness he directed operations. "I'd put a red ball there," he'd say, and then, "How 'bout a strip o' tinsel in that bare place?"

And every once in a while he'd cuddle up close to one of his new-found friends, and his whisper of joy would be almost piercingly sweet.

"It looks awful happy, the tree!" he'd whisper. "It looks awful happy—don't it?"

The situation—to the head stenographer—might have seemed unconventional. Under ordinary circumstances it would certainly have seemed more than unconventional to both the girl and the man. But conventions don't stand for much on the day before Christmas! As they worked together, laughing and joking, the Lonely Girl's prim hair spun itself into tiny curls across her forehead, and her eyes danced. And like a cloak the coldness slipped from the man who had also been lonely. They fell to talking, quite naturally, about the little intimate things of life that weren't very important and yet mattered infinitely much!

It wasn't strange that, along about tea time—when the shadows were just beginning to quiver over the floor—the little boy should fall suddenly asleep against the softness of the cushions. He wasn't used, you see, to so much excitement. It was then that the man and the girl, having covered him with a shawl, realized that they, too, were tired. And so the girl lighted a bayberry candle, and they sat down in the dusk together. And it was Christmas Eve!

"You know"—it was the man who spoke first—"you know, Miss Carleton, you've given me a great deal of pleasure today. Just letting me help." He paused, and his voice quivered ever so slightly. *It's been a long time since my soul has kept holiday!*"

The Lonely Girl—quite without meaning to—rested her fingers for a moment on the rough tweed of his coat sleeve. All at once words came fairly tumbling over each other, from her very heart. "It's hard, of course," she said, "for a man to be by himself in a huge city. But it's harder for a girl. I was used to a home, you see, and a mother. And—ever so long ago—a father. I used to hang up my stocking, and we had carols early Christmas morning. And there was turkey and plum pudding for dinner. I—I've missed it"—her voice faltered—"and today I was missing it more than ever, I think. If it hadn't been for the kiddie"—her gaze rested softly upon the little boy—"I would have been crying, this minute, with my head in a pillow!"

The man's voice was filled with a deep understanding. "I know," he said. "I'd not have been crying—but I know. People need company—and kiddies—at Christmas time. *And at every time.*"

There was a tremor in his tone that made the girl change the subject just a bit hurriedly.

"How," she questioned, "shall we manage a Santa Claus? We promised one, you know!"

The man was all enthusiasm. Had he ever really been a cool and detached person? "I've often thought that I'd like to play Santa to children of my own," he said, "and this youngster will be a mighty good substitute, bless him! See here—this is what we'll do: I'll take you all out to dinner. And I'll leave with a bunch of dandy excuses—about ice-cream time. I'll stop at a costumer's, and when you get back, Santa'll be here waiting."

There was a ring of youth—youth eternal—in his voice. And there was something else. It was the something else that made the girl cross the room suddenly to the sofa upon which the little boy was so peacefully sleeping.

"I wonder," she said slowly, "if you will stop at Mrs. Casey's and tell her that I'm keeping Benny overnight. Somehow I can't bear to let him go—before Christmas really comes!" She bent swiftly and kissed the child's flushed cheek.

They got to the first-name stage at the dinner table. The man's first name was Jim. And the Lonely Girl admitted to Nancy. She also admitted to other things.

"Do you know," she said, "that I thought you were a crabby old thing, once?"

"Do you know," the man answered, "that I never knew you were beautiful until this afternoon?"

At ice-cream time the party slowed up, just a bit, for the man left. But the little boy and the Lonely Girl had a wonderful white dessert with candied cherries set in stars around the top. And when it had all been devoured, as such desserts should be, they went back to the apartment. And a stout red and white Santa Claus—rather like a dessert himself—opened the door. And the little boy screamed with an excited indrawing of the breath, just as little boys and some grownups scream when a skyrocket goes up into the air.

There were gifts everywhere. It was as if the lonely, twisted tree had, in gratitude, blossomed. There were gifts that were sensible, such as shoes and mittens, and gifts that were utterly frivolous—such as mechanical toys and American Beauty roses. There was a marvelous electric train that wound on tracks all over the living room. It was while the girl and the little boy were busy adjusting the tracks of it that Santa Claus disappeared with never a word of farewell. And when, a few moments later, the man sauntered in, it was to find a little boy sobbing in the arms of a gloriously disheveled girl-woman.

"He lef'," the little boy was moaning, "an' I never told him what I wanted *most!*"

The girl was pressing the tired little head to her shoulder. "Why, honey," she sympathized, "I didn't know that there was anything else that you really wanted! Tell Nancy!"

The little boy's arms were flung suddenly around her neck. "I want *folks,*" sobbed the little boy, "of my own. Folks 'at won't mind because my back ain't straight. Folks 'at 'll love me—like I love my tree—an' not care!"

The man was leaning over the two of them. "I don't blame you, old fellow," he said, "for wanting folks. I want them myself. Santa Claus didn't bring me anything really important, either. He came when I was away. So you and I are in the same boat."

The crying of the little boy in no way diminished. His voice came up from the girl's shoulder in a muffled way.

"But you got each other!" he choked.

Suddenly, and with no idea at all of dramatics, the man was down on his knees in a clutter of tracks, beside them. Suddenly his arms were around their bodies.

"Oh, Nancy, have we?" he choked. "Have we got—each other?"

There was a glow in the girl's eyes—the glow that once looked out of the first woman's eyes in a garden place. But her words were of the child, when she spoke.

"Do you think that she'd let *us* have him?" she questioned, and she moved closer into his arms as she spoke. "Mrs. Casey, I mean?"

All at once the man was sobbing, himself. But the little boy was suddenly quiet, radiantly quiet.

In the corner the little lonely tree—lonely no longer—stood beaming proudly down upon them. Every colorful glass ball, every bird-shaped electric light, was like a separate chuckle. One, looking at it as it stood there, could hardly notice that it wasn't quite—straight.

The Third Rose

Joe L. Wheeler

The human heart defies description or analysis. What inner force attracts one person to another no psychologist has ever been able to tell us. The same is true of why such attraction comes and goes rather than remaining a constant.

The story of The Third Rose is one that has haunted me ever since I first heard it several years ago—and it has taken that long to write. Although it is honeycombed with twists, turns, blind alleys, and rabbit trails, through it all are three distinct paths well worth the following as they run parallel, merge, divide, merge, divide, with the passing of the years.

It is the story of two men, John and Walter, and the woman they both loved, Margaret—many years ago . . . once upon a war-time Christmas.

> Long years apart—can make no
> Breach a second cannot fill—
> The absence of the Witch does not
> Invalidate the spell—
>
> The embers of a Thousand Years
> Uncovered by the Hand
> That fondled them when they were Fire
> Will stir and understand.
> —Emily Dickinson

The surf was up at Point Arago on the Oregon coast . . . The surf was up all over the world.

It was December 17, 1941.

Only 10 days before, the Japanese had bombed Pearl Harbor. No American, child or adult, living then could possibly ever forget the static-plagued radio and the breaking voice of Edward R. Murrow; the broadcast sounds of antiaircraft guns, bombs, and explosions; sirens wailing up and down the auditory register like roller coasters on an eternal circular track; the heart-stopping whine of dive bombers plummeting full-throttle at sitting-duck targets below; and the pain-racked voice of Franklin Roosevelt declaring to millions clustered around radios that this was a date "which will live in infamy . . ." and, shortly afterward, that we were at war.

Forever after, these searing sounds, coupled with newsreel footage, newspaper and magazine illustrations depicting the carnage and sinking battleships, would separate the world that had been before from the world that came after.

It was a somber Christmas that year.

* * * * *

To all appearances, Margaret saw nothing . . . but woman's eyes are not man's eyes (merely seeing or not seeing); thus, filtered through those deceptively demure eyelashes was every nuance of the charade at the window. Two young men leaning against the window sill; one, she had known for years; the other, she had first met only hours before. They were both looking at

109

her, while pretending not to. John, with eyes luminous, tender, and possessive; Walter, conceding nothing, with eyes that challenged as clearly as if he had ripped off his knightly gage and hurled it to the floor only inches from her feet. Daring her to pick it up.

"This can't really be happening . . . this can't really be happening . . . this can't really be happening," she kept repeating to herself; "it must be just a dream." But it wasn't a dream; it was real—the realest thing that had ever happened to her.

"But . . . how *could* it have happened?" she demanded of the faithless doorkeeper of her heart. For it was all but settled: she and John. Six years, it had been; six years of thoughtful attentiveness, steadfast devotion, and empathetic understanding. John was the kindest boy, the kindest man, she had ever known. He was the only one of her many suitors through the years who was more concerned with her inner journey than his own; encouraging her to follow her dreams, wherever they led, no matter how long the road.

How paradoxical, she mused, that out of all this world such a man could be. No one else had ever been intrepid enough to embark on such a long and arduous quest: searching behind the lovely facade for the shy little spirit huddled deep within, in a chamber only she had ever seen. His "Holy Grail," he termed it when she laughingly declared it didn't exist.

Margaret was both grateful and frightened by this quest: on one hand, she was deeply moved that he cared enough to make such a long and possibly unrewarding journey; on the other hand, she was not at all sure that she wanted to know this much about her inner self—

and even, in a rather perverse way, resented his forcing her to unlock doors she wasn't sure she wanted unlocked. After all, women of her day were still "whither thou goest, I will go"; few indeed staked out career claims in the male-dominated world of 1941 America. She had no way of knowing—so many thousands of women would enter the work force during the next four years—that by the time the veterans returned to reclaim their jobs, it would prove impossible to ever stuff women back into their claustrophobic boxes.

She had known for months that he was closing in— and she both dreaded and yearned for his coming. And then . . . he stumbled on the cobwebby secret passage to her soul's innermost chamber. Wearily, he cleared a path to her door, paused to regain his breath, then— ever so gently—knocked.

For so long had this vault been hers alone that she trembled like an aspen during a storm at the soft knock. When he softly knocked again, she pushed open the massive steel door . . . a slit.

And there he stood, demanding nothing, asking nothing, not knowing even then if he would be turned away.

It was this very absence of force that decided her: she leaned all her weight into the door . . . and welcomed him in.

* * * * *

To John and Margaret, poetry was meat and drink, the medium by which their intertwining souls could soar, their minds to expand, and their hearts to open wide.

Longfellow provided patriotism and the homely virtues; Wordsworth, the continuity of life; Tennyson, its romance; Dickinson, the cosmic view; from Arnold, a sense of restraint; from Frost, a perception of choices; and from Robinson, empathy—but it was Yeats who unrolled for them Life's long carpet, from beginning to end.

Paradoxically, however, in all this, John's own self-awareness lagged far behind; in fact, it took almost six years for him to wake up to his true condition. For Margaret, that knowledge had come much earlier; thanks to her intuition (God's kindest and cruelest gift to woman), she knew that he loved her, and that some day soon he would tell her so.

It came unexpectedly, on a balmy November day on Bandon Beach. One of those rare, absolutely perfect, days life parts with so grudgingly. Serenely, Autumn held her ground, staring fixedly out to sea; while northward, beyond the mountains, Winter kept shaking his watch, scowling at the delay.

Hand in hand, John led Margaret away from the sea's edge to their favorite sand dune, and enthroned her there. Self-consciously, he opened a well-worn book and turned to a certain page. Then, his face aglow with more than he knew, he recited, without once looking at the page, Yeats' haunting "When You Are Old." It seemed to her both bizarre and oddly touching, in the morning of her beauty, to be the recipient of such lines as these:

When you are old and gray and full of sleep,
And nodding by the fire, take down this book,

And slowly read, and dream of the soft look
Your eyes had once, and of their shadows deep;

How many loved your moments of glad grace,
And loved your beauty with love false or true,
But one man loved the pilgrim soul in you,
And loved the sorrows of your changing face;

And bending down beside the glowing bars,
Murmur, a little sadly, how Love fled
And paced upon the mountains overhead
And hid his face among a crowd of stars.

"Pilgrim" was ever after that his pet name for her—and the sea-framed image of her long dark tresses blowing westward in the wind was etched for all time on his heart.

The moment was that rarity, a twin epiphany—for her, a bittersweet revelation of the ephemeral nature of beauty, love, and life; for him, the first realization that he was in love with her. As he reached those memorable seventh and eighth lines, a wave of scarlet flooded his face. Both instinctively knew, in that moment, that something had come to an end, something had begun—and nothing would ever be the same.

* * * * *

Yesterday, as she and John had walked hand in hand, barefoot on the beach, her heart had met his more than halfway. Both were children of the sea, never happier than when freed from chores, school, work, and family, to wander at will down their sandy heaven, feel-

ing themselves a symbiotic part of the eternal romance of sand and sea.

She knew then, without a shadow of a doubt, that sometime this Christmas he would ask that crucial question that determines earthly destiny more than any other—and her love-lit sea-blue eyes telegraphed what her answer would be.

Yet . . . she had stumbled once on a slippery rock, and he had opportunistically taken her in his arms. That almost certainly would have precipitated the moment had she let nature take its course. But, for some strange inexplicable reason, she had gently disengaged. Something within her warned, "Not yet."

But all that was yesterday. Yesterday? *Only yesterday?* But the world had changed last night!

Last September, her sister Beatrice had written her about a young man, Walter, who had just transferred to the parochial college she attended in Northern California. He was a senior theology major and so irresistible that most of the girls on campus melted at the sight of him. Apparently, he had every talent and gift the good Lord could give: his wit was rapier-sharp, his mind was second to none, his smile would cause a nun to repent her vows, he could sing like Sankey and preach like Moody—when he had finished a sermon, dry eyes were a vanished species. For good measure, Walter had a wickedly irresistible sense of humor and the kind of looks and physique Michelangelo would have traveled far to capture in Carrara marble.

"But so far," rhapsodized Beatrice," this paragon has not succumbed to the open invitations in the admiring eyes of so many campus beauties. The question everyone is asking is, 'Who in the world is he *waiting* for?'"

Beatrice, already signed, sealed, and delivered to Anthony, Walter's best friend, had become personally acquainted with the "campus dreamboat" (so designated by no less than the campus newspaper). On an October picnic at the Old Mill in Napa Valley, Walter made the mistake of wandering over to where Beatrice sat enshrined, in a stone cleft, by the towering water wheel. To the music of the slumbering water cascading listlessly into the amber pond, they got to know each other better. For Beatrice, an incurable matchmaker, to have passed up such an opportunity as this would have been grossly out of character. On the spur of this autumn moment, she entered another candidate into the lists: her sister Margaret. Why she did such a thing, she was never afterward able to explain to her husband, for both of them dearly loved John and had, for some time, accepted him as their brother-in-law-to-be.

Whatever the reason for her mischief, once started she fired every cannon on her ship. She described her sister's beauty, vivacious personality, irresistible smile, pixieish sense of humor, good figure, bookwormishness, poise, wanderlust, and—for good measure—her close walk with the Lord.

When she had fired her last shell, Walter laughed as he hadn't in months, causing everyone within a mile to wonder what in the world had happened to *him*. "What a set-up!" he finally managed to say. "No woman could be *that* perfect!" Nevertheless, the damage was done: he now *had* to find out for himself, harassing the not-overly reluctant Beatrice until she finally broke down and invited him home with them for Christmas. He accepted, on condition that he provide the transportation.

Along the way, in his sporty new Buick, he pumped both Beatrice and Anthony for additional tidbits of information. Anthony, having had second and third thoughts by this time, was beginning to regret the whole thing as he conceptualized what effect bringing "Dreamboat" home with them was likely to have on the all-but-engaged Margaret and John. To him, bringing Walter home was tantamount to giving a lion free rein in a hen house.

By now, even Beatrice was realizing the fuller implications of what she had done, the forces she was setting in motion. If she could have recaptured those more-enticing-than-she-had-planned-on words at the Old Mill, she would have—but it was too late. This particular lion had never in his life taken no for an answer if he really wanted something. Perhaps . . . oh, pray God, perhaps . . . he wouldn't be any more impressed with her than he was with the coeds back on campus.

Beatrice, sitting between the two men, mused, *John is the type of man most women in their 30s would choose to marry and father their children, but not—not women in their late teens and early 20s. What have I DONE!* she cried out to herself.

Anthony, knowing even before he opened his mouth that his warnings would have no more effect than a garden hose against a volcano, told Walter that his sister-in-law was as good as engaged to a young man the whole family loved. This line of reasoning was just a tad short of being inspired as he should have known that Walter, being Walter, would only be more intrigued: he valued only more the things he was told he couldn't have.

At last they crossed the state line into Oregon, chugged up and over the Siskiyou Pass, and began their long descent to the coast. Even though war had been declared, towns they passed through had a festive air about them. It would be, after all, a Christmas to remember when the boys were gone—many, never to return.

Reaching the coastal road at last, they turned north toward Coos Bay; finally, they could see, way up on the hill, the large two-story home that dominated everything between the forest and the highway: HOME. Walter turned off onto a long gravel road, then circled up and around to the back of the house, where he cut the engine.

Anthony and Beatrice went in first, and were promptly engulfed by the family. Belatedly they remembered their driver, still waiting in the anteroom, and went after him.

Walter was escorted into the homey living room in a state of intense expectancy. Never in his life had his anticipations been so high. Four of Beatrice's five sisters were in the room waiting for them. Mama, the only other person who knew what was afoot, had sent Margaret off for a walk—knowing John would follow—as soon as her eagle eye had spied Walter's car turn into the long driveway. She, too, loved John—almost, in fact, as much as Papa did.

Walter, not in on Mama's diversionary tactics, kept searching for the sister who would answer to the de-

scription. As each sister—Daphne, Christina, Melissa, and Jasmine—was introduced, each attractive in her own way, his spirits rose and fell.

Thirty of the longest minutes in Walter's lifetime later, Margaret and John slipped back into the house. Beatrice, having reached the long delayed moment of truth, stumblingly went through the introductions, hoping against hope that Walter would be a good boy and let her off the hook. Instead, there occurred what she had most feared, an explosion of awareness generated by the two.

All Margaret did was smile. But that five-letter-word hardly did justice to a weapon that had already bewitched the entire male population of the county. Papa (who certainly ought to have known, since it had been used with such unfailing success on him) had summed it up best: "That deadly smile of hers is both impish and demure. How in God's green earth can mortal man resist a combination like that?"

Walter broke no records in that respect. He was poleaxed, not even having the saving grace to hide his condition. The rest of that eventful evening passed in sort of a roseate haze for the principals. They spoke occasionally to each other in mere words . . . but almost continually with their eyes.

Rhetorically, Margaret asked herself, *Why is there a veil over my response to John, to the open love-light in his eyes, to that tenderness that only hours ago represented all that I most wanted in life?*

John, so attuned to her every vibration or nuance, sensed the difference immediately. Already he sensed a withdrawing of her inner spirit (that Pilgrim he had searched for so many years, before finding)—and he was deeply troubled.

Later that night, John trudged up the creaking stairs to the attic aerie where he always slept when visiting Margaret. Despondently, he reviewed the day's events and asked himself what he could have said or done differently to change the outcome. As he lay down wearily on the cot by the window, he felt he had somehow been battered black and blue during the evening. He looked out through the window, as he always did at night, down to the coastal highways where ghostly headlights in the fog searched for passage to somewhere. Always before, this bed had represented home (for once he had come to know Margaret, it had been inconceivable that home could ever be anywhere but next to her). But now he had a chilling sense of being evicted, that he was going to be thrown out onto that foggy highway himself . . . to begin another search for he knew not what. Certainly he could not even imagine another woman.

As for Walter, he had gone to bed almost in a state of shock. Well he knew how unutterably dear Margaret was to John. In fact, "dear" was the ultimate understatement. She was his whole world, and every time he looked at her, his undiluted love was unmistakable. But he knew also that were John the dearest male friend he had ever known, he could not possibly surrender the field short of the altar. Dimly he began to realize that love is the most powerful force on earth. When it comes in full strength, nothing—no person, no matter how close a friend—can stand in the way. The drama has to be played out.

Margaret, too, found sleep very elusive. Her sisters had given her a hard time, for they loved John like the brother they had lost so many years before. Heretofore they had assumed the certainty of his brother-in-lawhood. Nevertheless, they knew their sister well enough to realize that this complete stranger, in one short evening, had pulverized her almost impregnable defense system. Margaret, loving John deeply, was furious with herself for her patent inability to hold Walter at bay; she was equally angry with Walter for wrecking what should have been the happiest Christmas of her lifetime.

For most of that interminable night she wrestled with her terrible dilemma. Face it: she loved them both—but in totally different ways.

The next morning, all three were slow in reappearing— and when they did, the night's toll was painfully obvious.

The stand-off continued day after day, with most of the rounds seemingly won by John, for Margaret respected his right to be first in her company. But the victory was somewhat hollow, for John felt himself now only partly in possession of her love. When they were alone, he felt he had two-thirds of her, but when Walter was in the room it was an entirely different story. He could feel the aerial shock waves as the inner spirits of Walter and Margaret challenged each other, communed with each other, longed for each other.

It was the twenty-fourth of December when it finally came: the denouement. Long into the previous night, Walter tossed and turned, unable to find sleep.

He candidly took stock of the situation and concluded that things didn't look very good for him; here he was, nearing the time when he'd have to return to college, and he was getting nowhere. Should he leave without a decision in his favor, he felt confident that the combined forces of family preference and John's residence in that part of the state would eventually break down the last of Margaret's resistance. Only with a bold stroke did he have a fighting chance. But all his life he would be known for such risk-taking; it was his willingness to seize the moment and take control that would make him a millionaire before he was 30.

At breakfast, John was sitting next to Margaret as usual, and beginning to feel that the tide was at last beginning to shift in his favor. Somehow, Margaret's smile promised more than it had yesterday. Perhaps . . . all was not lost after all.

Across the table, Walter was reaching the same conclusion. There was not a moment to lose. As they got up from the table, his voice cut through the babble of voices and moving chairs: "Margaret, could I speak with you for a moment?" All action and speech froze in mid air.

He led Margaret into the front parlor, her face changing color as she walked. *It's coming!* she couldn't help thinking. But she had underestimated Walter—he was not going to accept any front parlor odds if he could help it.

Within two minutes he pulled off what proved to be the greatest selling job of his long and illustrious career—he persuaded her that she owed him a few minutes alone with her. Since they both loved the sea, and since it was such an absolutely perfect morning, and since he was leaving so soon—as he had hoped, her face blanched as he spoke these words—surely she would grant him this one small favor: take a short ride to the beach with him. Smilingly, she allowed that perhaps it might be arranged.

Walter went out to spruce up the car and warm the engine. From inside he overheard loud voices: Papa was apparently most unhappy about something. More time passed. More voices. This time it was Mama, apparently trying to mediate. Almost he felt he had lost . . . then she came flying out of the house . . . her face flushed. Signs of recent tears confirmed his suspicion that her exit had not been an easy one. The car was already rolling as she lightly slipped aboard.

When Margaret had informed John that she would be gone a short while with Walter—wasn't it sweet of him to take her for a ride to the beach in his shiny new Buick?—John was under no illusions as to the mettle of his antagonist. In 1941 America, it just wasn't done for a guy to take another's steady (especially an all but affianced one!) off in an automobile alone. Not in conservative Christian families, it wasn't.

If Walter could pull this off in two minutes . . . then just give him sole possession for a few hours, especially with this particular woman—and at the beach, for good measure. Short of a miracle, the game was lost. Worst of all, he wasn't even being permitted to be on the scene; all he could do was worry and fear the worst.

The hours inched their way on crippled feet across that fateful day. Everything in the two-story home stalled to a virtual halt as family members tried to avoid meeting each other's eyes, *especially* John's, so brimming with misery (he always *did* wear his heart in his eyes). The morning hours passed and afternoon came. Papa kept looking at his watch and muttering things. Mama kept out of range whenever possible.

Late in the afternoon, as evening shadows fell, the one-two slam of car doors ricocheted through the silent house. Faces froze for the interminable period it took Margaret and Walter to climb the long set of outside steps, open the front door, and walk through the front parlor into the inner one. And then: the verdict.

Every eye was riveted on the couple—every eye but John's. Heaven and hell were no further away than one glance at Margaret . . . so he preferred to remain suspended between.

Her voice had bells in it, bells of joy that no cloud of mere words could ever counter. Bells that tolled the death of all his dreams . . . for what was the use of anything without Margaret there to share it with him?

Across the room, Papa's face had hardened into cold gray stone—for in his heart, he had long ago adopted John as the son he always longed for, since his own had died an untimely death. And Mama's face ignited with waves of burning pain, for she too had long loved John—with all the intensity of a sonless mother. The five sisters just sat there . . . for the first time in living memory . . . all silent at once.

Walter, in the egocentricity of youth, thought only of his own rapture, scarcely giving a second thought to the one he had displaced.

As Margaret read in the faces of those around her the impact of her decision, the bells ceased to ring in her voice. Well she knew how John must be feeling. She could read it in the anguish etched in his face, the abject slump of his body, and the unspoken thoughts that always arced between them—even without words. She knew all this but could do nothing about it, for the very reasons Beatrice had feared: her standards of evaluation were those of the young—they who worship power, success, charisma, physical prowess, looks, and passion.

Walter had it all. John, on the other hand, was unfortunate enough to embody traits women don't appreciate until the traumas of the years reshuffle their priorities. His were the gifts of tenderness, empathy, understanding, introspection, sensitivity, serenity, and imagination.

Through swollen eyelids on that never-to-be-forgotten Christmas Eve, John watched paradise recede from him. Margaret still went through the motions, still attempted to include him—but both knew it was a sham. The heart, that unpredictable instrument, had shifted its center of gravity 180 degrees. One moment, John represented the perceived future; another moment, he did not. There were no ragged edges: it was a clean break.

On Margaret's face was that inward glow that illuminates a woman during that ever-so-short blooming period we label, for want of a better phrase, "falling in love."

It was the last night John ever spent in that house. In the morning, on her bureau was a single long-stemmed red rose, and leaning against the stem, an envelope. It was the first thing Margaret saw when she awoke from a troubled sleep. Quickly, she slipped out of bed with a radiant smile spreading across her sleepy face—then stopped in dismay, her hands flying to her ghost-white cheeks. The writing was John's, not Walter's.

Even before she opened it she knew it was the end of something that only days before had embodied her fondest dreams. The note was short. The shortest one he had ever written her.

Dec. 25, 1941

My dearest Margaret,

It is clearly over.

Yet, if you should change your mind, just send me a red rose, signing the card "Pilgrim," and I shall come to you if it be in my power to do so.

I shall always love you.

John

Margaret's sisters awoke to the sound of weeping, the most tempestuous sobbing they had ever heard from their sunny sister. When asked what it was all about, she could only point mutely to the note and rose. Each read it, looked at her pensively, and quietly left the room. This was *her* battle, *her* decision, and she would have to live with the consequences for the rest of her life.

* * * * *

118

Margaret and Walter were married the first day of May.

The years swept by on winged feet. Margaret and Walter were about as happy as husband and wife ever are on this troubled planet. Walter had the Midas touch: everything he touched turned to gold. During the war years, he made a fortune; in after years, he merely augmented it.

If ever a man lived life in the fast lane, it was Walter. Being with him, Margaret soon discovered, was a perpetual adventure, for he lived with Falstaffian gusto. Fast cars, fast boats, and fast planes—he was ever on the move, always making deals that were ever more lucrative than those that went before.

He tried everything: preacher, teacher, auctioneer, real estate salesman, politician, entrepreneur, and all-around tycoon . . . filling each role with incredible energy, joie de vivre, and robust laughter.

And Margaret was his Guinevere, the mistress of his splendid homes, villas, and mountain resorts. With Walter she was able to satisfy her yearning for travel . . . and that always in luxury, always first class.

They had everything money could buy—yet somehow both retained the common touch, selflessly giving to those less fortunate. In spite of many temptations, he remained faithful to her—and to the Lord, who remained paramount in their lives.

Only one child survived—and so excruciating was that second delivery that he swore never to inflict another pregnancy upon her.

Never once did Walter give Margaret cause to regret having chosen him instead of John, who seemingly had dropped off the planet. In all their long years together, never once did they hear whether or not John had survived the war.

But John *did* make it through; rather perversely, fate brought him safely through battles he hoped to die in. Gradually, over time, he rediscovered his lost love of life and literature. And just before the Battle of Guadalcanal, he invited God back into his life.

After the war was over, he took stock of his options, and determined that he would not permit the loss of Margaret to destroy his life. Taking advantage of the GI Bill he went back to college and earned a degree in architecture. Increasingly lonely, he began to search for someone to spend the rest of his life with. Several years later, he found her. And she was everything he had hoped she would be.

Three children came their way . . . and life was good.

* * * * *

It seemed impossible that *anything* could slow the juggernaut of Walter's life and his far-flung involvements and enterprises—but it happened, nevertheless. Three days after their forty-third wedding anniversary, he was diagnosed as having cancer—both terminal and fast-spreading.

Five weeks later, on a spring afternoon, he asked Margaret to push his bed over to the large picture window that overlooked San Francisco Bay and the Golden Gate Bridge. The sun was setting, gilding the blue into bronze. A sleek ocean liner (one they had traveled on several times) had just cleared the bridge and was head-ing out to sea. He sighed audibly . . . and she knew what he was thinking.

Life is such an overconscientious accountant, mused Margaret to herself. *When one is given the world on a silver platter, the reckoning tends to come earlier. Here is Walter, at the very height of his powers, and suddenly it's all over. Why, oh why, God?*

She sensed that he had turned and was looking at her. The look in his dear hazel eyes was more than she could handle: the look that told her that, after all the long years, she was still . . . *everything.*

He took her hands in his . . . she could feel him trembling—from way down deep inside. "Don't cry, dear," he said in his now rather ragged voice as he searched for the Kleenex box. "Don't cry. We've had it all. I've been lucky—far luckier than most—in that most all of my dreams have come true. There isn't much I wanted to do . . . which I haven't. . . . Don't let them give me one of those idiotic sentimental funerals when I go—or let Diane do it either. By the way, where *is* she?"

"Went down to Safeway for some groceries, dear. She'll be right back."

"Oh . . . Dear . . . promise me there will be no funeral. Just cremate what little there is left of me"—he looked down ruefully at his emaciated body, comparing it to what had been—"and have it carried out to sea, way out beyond the Golden Gate, and dropped overboard. So when you wish to think of me, just walk down to the shore, as you so love to do . . . and listen to 'em coming in. I'll be out there somewhere—my spirit will . . . in whatever form the good Lord packages it . . ."

He paused so long she thought he had dropped off

to sleep. But no, he had only been thinking—about her. There was that tender look again in his eyes . . . which remained in full strength even while his body was savaged by wave after wave of pain. "Any regrets, dear," he asked, "any regrets at all?"

"NONE!" she responded instantly. "Oh, Walter, if I had it to do all over again . . ." and her eyes—her still-impish eyes—twinkled wickedly through tears. She could see his face visibly relax, and a smile struggled against the only force he had ever been unable to outwit.

Those were his last words . . . and he died with that smile on his face.

And she was alone.

* * * * *

Several long years passed . . . and life began to regain its savor. To take her mind off her loss, Margaret resumed her volunteer stints at the local hospital. She also resumed her traveling to the far corners of the earth. Often she would book passage with her sister Melissa, just to have someone with her to keep the loneliness in check.

Then it happened. . . . At a family celebration in a distant California city, she happened to sit behind a man who looked vaguely familiar. Then he turned and spoke to the woman at his side—and she *knew!* Her stupefied "JOHN!" escaped her before she could check it, causing him to turn around and look at her. He knew her instantly. He introduced his wife, Phyllis; and Margaret introduced her daughter, Diana. They spoke only briefly, Margaret finding herself strangely tongue-tied. Then John turned around and faced the front again. The program went on without her—for all that she could see in her blurred vision was that dear face now hidden from her. For the first time in 47 years she knew he was alive. ALIVE!

As long as Walter had been alive, so dominant was he that the force field of energy that he generated blotted out thoughts of all who were not part of his personal galaxy. Hence, during all those rushing years rarely had the pace of life slowed enough for much introspection. But now, with that dynamo quiet, cold, and silent, memories flooded back upon her, compounded with 47 years of interest, as if a towering dam had buckled under irresistible pressure and unleashed with a vengeance the no longer placid waters imprisoned behind. In such torrents did they engulf her that she stood to her feet, dazed, and left the family celebration without being able to explain her untimely exit to anyone, even her astonished daughter. The only rational thought that filtered through this deluge brought her anything but peace: AFTER ALL THESE YEARS, THE FIRE STILL BURNS!

She returned to her life, only now she was lonelier than ever. Hungry again, but not hungry for Walter. That part of her life had come and gone like a gigantic meteor, utterly all-consuming, igniting the sky with its radiance. When such a shooting star burns out, no one who has lived with it for long could possibly desire a second ride. Flesh and blood can handle such an experience only once in life.

She was reminded of Elijah: after the whirlwind came the still, the small, the quiet, voice.

So it was that, after all those sonic years, she yearned . . . she longed . . . for John. But now . . . it was too late. Too late.

Now she used travel—not as the joy it had always been before . . . but as an escape. An escape from memories of John. She now rarely came home, but could be found instead in Nepal, in Bali, in the Australian Outback, in Patagonia, in Dubrovnik on the Dalmatian Coast, in the foggy Aleutians, in the Bay Islands . . . always moving on, in an effort to forget.

One humid tropical afternoon, as she fanned herself on the hotel balcony in Papeete, Tahiti, the maître d' brought her a letter on a tray. It was from her daughter.

November 12, 1991

Dear Mother,
Your grandchildren are growing up without you. Wouldn't you like to be there for them before it's too late?
By the way, just heard that the wife of your old sweetheart died of cancer. A year ago, I believe.

Much love,
Diana

Two days later, she was home.
Now it was even worse, for there was no longer any human barrier separating her from John. But would he, after all these years, still be interested in her? Would he so resent her rejection of him that he'd refuse to have anything to do with her? After almost half a century, could he possibly still care for her in the old way? If he *did* still care, why hadn't he written her?

The weeks passed and her composure continued to unravel strand by strand: she was rapidly degenerating into a nervous wreck. True, she had, by some diligent sleuthing, managed to secure his address. But she was of the old school, not the new one. Thus she did not dare take the initiative herself. She called her daughter and asked for advice. Instead, she was invited to come visit that weekend.

That Saturday evening, looking out at the multicolored Christmas lights decorating houses and yards across the way, listening to carols on radio and CDs, her thoughts wafted back once again to that wonderful/terrible Christmas of '41. Mama—long since dead; the same with Papa. Now it was just the six sisters left—and the oldest would almost certainly not make another Christmas.

Suddenly, the voice of her daughter broke into her reveries: "Mother, I've been wracking my brain, trying to think of some way you could contact your John without violating the quaint ol' code your generation was plagued with. Why, today"—and she chuckled diabolically—"today, your granddaughter would most likely have abducted him by now."

She had to laugh at her mother's crimson face. "Why, Mother, you can still blush! It's been a long time since I've seen anyone blush. Today, we are shocked so often, and at such a young age, and we are bombarded with so much sexual innuendo, that we are shock-proof. No one blushes anymore."

She went on. "Mother, didn't he leave any ragged edges—any open ends you could take advantage of? Or was it a surgical cut—" She stopped suddenly as her mother's hands flew to her face. "Mother, what *is* it?"

"Oh, I just remembered . . . no, it was anything but a surgical cut. How could I have possibly forgotten! He . . . he . . . uh . . . left me a rose the morning he left, Christmas morning. What a present! I cried like I never had before, or have since. A rose . . . and . . . a note."

"Go on. Go on!" commanded Diana.

Her mother paused, and a dreamy look came into her eyes as she was swept back through the years. Diana thought to herself, *It must have been that look that captured those two so very different hearts. Mother is still beautiful. Imagine, just imagine what she must have been like then. And ALL WOMAN.*

"'My dearest Margaret.'" Here Margaret's eyes filled with tears, and she could go no further. After some time, she regained her composure. "I had just . . . uh . . . jilted him . . . and he . . . he . . .still . . . called . . . me . . . 'dearest.' I had never thought of that before."

Diana waited.

Finally, her mother was able to proceed. "'My dearest Margaret. . . . It is . . . uh . . . clearly over.'" She paused, a stricken look in her eyes: "Oh it was, it WAS," she wailed, "but it's not, oh pray God it's NOT!"

After a while, she continued: "'Yet . . . if you should change your mind . . . just send me a . . . a red rose . . . , signing the card "Pilgrim" . . .'" She paused, and

explained, "That was his pet name for me. At home . . . I still have that book of Yeats poems. When I moved into my small seashore home after Walter died, it was one of the few things I just couldn't bear to part with. I . . . I mean WE . . . used to eat, drink, and sleep poetry. But through the years . . . uh . . . well, as you know, your father never liked poetry very much . . . and so he discouraged me from reading it—so I didn't. But I could now . . . I CAN now!"

Diana pounced: "Mother! You never told me. But, of course, I never asked. . . . But, come to think of it, you were Dad's queen, weren't you . . . Just as I was his princess. But you were the crown jewel of his kingdom. But . . . but . . . before Dad died, I never really knew you as a person . . . like me . . . with drives . . . and dreams . . . of your own."

Her mother didn't answer. She didn't have to.

"Mother, tell me more about that pet name he had for you, 'Pilgrim.' That, in a strangely beautiful way, seems to fit you. But how did he tie it into—what did you say the writer's name was?"

"Yeats." And again that tender softness came back into her eyes. *The look of a Raphael madonna*, Diana thought to herself. *That's not a look one sees much today.*

"Pilgrim." Her mother's mouth curved adorably as she formed the word. "He said I was his pilgrim. We both memorized the poem."

"Can you, after all these years, still remember any of the lines?"

"Let's see." She paused, wrinkling her forehead. Finally, in exasperation, she sighed: "I just can't seem to remember. I do remember that Yeats begins by telling his beloved that when she is old—oh! I am old now, aren't I! When she is old and thinking back to when she wasn't, when she was still . . ."

"Beautiful?"

"Yes. Beautiful . . . Wait! I do remember that one middle stanza. The one that told him he was in love with me."

"Well, let's hear it quickly . . . before you forget."

"I won't forget . . ."

How many loved your moments of glad grace,
And loved your beauty with love false or true,
But one man loved the pilgrim soul in you
And loved the sorrows of your changing face.

As she came to the last words of the stanza, Margaret broke down completely, her tears falling unchecked like silver rain.

Diana just sat there, quietly, a pensive look on her face. This was a mother she had never known before. Where had she been all these years?

At last, the tears spent, her mother looked up, saying, as she dabbed her eyes, "You must think I'm such a silly fool."

"No," responded Diana slowly. "Never have I loved—or admired—you more. . . . Was that all of it?"

"All of what? Oh, you mean the letter?"

"Of COURSE."

"Not quite. Come to think of it, a rather big 'quite.'"

"Oh?"

"Yes. Let's see, where did I leave off?"

"Pilgrim." I believe you said 'pilgrim soul.'"

"Oh, yes . . . 'Just send me a red rose, signing the card 'Pilgrim' . . . and I shall return to you if it be . . .'" and here she paused for control . . . "'if it be . . . in my power to do so.'"

"Was that all?"

"No. A thousand times NO! He ended with these six words . . . 'I shall always love you . . . John.'"

"Do you think he really meant them?"

"YES! Meant them then. Yes. But the big question is . . . is . . ."

"Whether or not he still does today?"

In an almost inaudible whisper, her mother answered, "Yes."

* * * * *

It was the twenty-first day of December.

John stood in the front room of his modest split-level home in the Oregon highlands, gazing absent-mindedly out at the falling snow and snow-flocked pines. Christmas alone. . . . He just didn't know how he could handle it again. Oh, of course, the children had invited him home to be with their families, but somehow he just couldn't seem to get in the mood for that kind of Christmas.

Well, to be truthful, it was more than that.

He was living more and more in the past these days, it seemed. Phyllis was already part of the past, which could no longer be changed. She had come into his life when he needed her most . . . and stayed until her life forces failed her, as, sooner or later, they do for all of us. But she was gone, never to return. As Frost's persona put it in his poem "Out, Out—"

> Little—less—nothing—and that ended it.
> No more to build on there.

"No more to build on there." In fact, he asked himself, was there anything or anyone to build on at all? Was his life over?

The raucous ring—really, he must change that thing!—of the doorbell jerked him out of his dream world. Who could be calling on a day like this? He certainly wasn't in the mood for company, he growled to himself, as he pulled open the door.

A florist delivery boy was standing there, the snow already frosting his blond head.

After signing for the slim package, he closed the door in relief. At least he would not be forced to leave his journey into the past in order to talk about things that mattered less and less to him . . . Oh, the package. Wonder who it could be from. As for the "what," older people don't get very excited about that, for they have everything already, and are far more concerned about having to part with something they already have than they are anxious to receive something new.

He opened it. In the narrow box was one of the loveliest red roses he had ever seen. He lifted it out of the box with arthritic hands, and inhaled its fragrance. Then, wondering who it could be from, poked around in the green tissue paper until he found a small white envelope. He opened it.

His eyes widened in disbelief as he read the message on the card. It consisted of but one word:

PILGRIM

On the back of the card there was no name—but there was an address and phone number.

*****

The twenty-third day of December.

Margaret's heart was racing like a cold engine on a frosty morning. Two entire days had passed—and she had heard nothing. Had she been a silly old ninny to imagine John would still be interested in her? An old woman with precious few good years left.

She leaned against her bedroom window and gazed idly out at a sight she never tired of: the booming surf off Point Lobos. One of Walter's last gifts to her had been this little hideaway overlooking one of the grandest views on this planet. Since no more land was available on this stretch of Seventeen Mile Drive, he had probably bought off half of the California legislature, and paid a king's ransom for it to boot. Wisely, she had asked no questions, just accepted it as his Taj Mahal, the ultimate gift to the woman he adored.

She leaned against the window and spoke with God. Always, she had maintained a child-like faith in Him. And her prayers were rarely formal things; rather, they were as casual as if she were merely chatting with a friend in the room. This one was typical in that respect:

> Oh, God, have I done it again? Did I move
> too quickly . . . before I had Your blessing?
> But oh, Lord, I am so lonely . . . and John was
> so good to me all those years ago when I was

young. But that's what worries me, God. Will he still think I am pretty today? What do You think, God?

She looked out the window again and noticed that the fog was coming in—and the gulls were protesting.

She jumped as the telephone shattered the stillness. It was the gateman. "Sorry to disturb you, ma'am, but a package just came for you. The man who delivered it declared it urgent; said it *had* to get to you today. Shall I bring it up?"

Within minutes, he was at her door with it (on the long box was the engraved imprint of her favored Carmel florist). The gateman thanked, the door shut with almost impolite haste, and the box opened with shaking fingers, she beheld three perfect red roses. But she refused to pick them up until she found out who they were from, and what the message was.

Her normally nimble fingers had a little trouble finding the small envelope; then, ever so carefully, she opened it—*almost*, she quipped to herself, *as if I thought a bomb would explode when I opened it.*

On a small sheet of stationery were these words:

Dearest Pilgrim,
Second Rose received; am returning. First Rose long since dead; am sending replacement. Third Rose to present my case—and Emily:
"Where Roses would not dare to go,
What Heart would risk the way—
And so I send my Crimson Scouts
To sound the Enemy—"

If they are persuasive enough, I'll see you at Bandon Beach, Dec. 25, 9:00 a.m., in vicinity of Yeats Sand Dune.

Until then—
Your John

* * * * *

It was Christmas morning on Bandon Beach.
At 9:00 on the second, a tall graceful woman descended the stairs leading down to the beach. The roses of youth were in her cheeks, and pinned to her breast was a corsage of three crimson roses.

At the bottom of the stairs, she kicked off her shoes.

After rounding the huge rock, she saw him, standing by a sand dune that looked vaguely familiar.

When she got close enough to read his eyes—
and see his open arms—
she broke into a run.
Pilgrim had come home.

Long years apart can make no
Breach a second cannot fill—
The absence of the Witch does not
Invalidate the spell.

The embers of a Thousand Years
Uncovered by the Hand
That fondled them when they were Fire
Will stir and understand.
—Emily Dickinson

125

Emily Dickinson, "Long Years Apart," Poem
    1383, *The Complete Poems of Emily Dickinson*.
    Written c. 1876.
————, "Where Roses Would Not Dare to
    Go," Poem 1582, *The Complete Poems of
    Emily Dickinson*. Written c. 1883.
William Butler Yeats, "When You Are Old,"
    The Rose. 1893.